"I'm not saying we should act as if nothing happened. To tell you the truth, we _can't_."

"What do you mean?"

Lily's insides were already churning with crazy feelings of hope mingled with anxiety. Seeing Bastian again, the last...the very _last_ thing she could do was pretend indifference to the situation.

"Are you trying to tell me that there's someone else on the scene? Is that why you want to forget about what happened?"

The affront in his voice took her aback. Tucking a stray strand of pale gold hair back into her bun where it had drifted free, it wasn't easy to keep her hands from trembling. "There isn't anyone else...and I can hardly forget what happened when—"

"When what?" He leaned forward, his hands on his knees as if immediately ready to spring to his feet and confront anything he found remotely disagreeable.

Understandably nervous, her heart racing like a greyhound's out of the trap, Lily lifted her head and bravely met the Italian's glowering stare. This was no time to give way to fear, she told herself.

"When I find myself expecting your baby."

Maggie Cox is passionate about stories that can uplift and transport people out of their daily worries to a more magical place, be they romance novels or fairy tales. What people want most, she believes, is true connection. She feels blessed to be married to a lovely man who never fails to make her laugh, and has two beautiful sons and two much-loved grandchildren.

Books by Maggie Cox

Harlequin Presents

Required to Wear the Tycoon's Ring
A Rule Worth Breaking
The Man She Can't Forget
The Tycoon's Delicious Distraction
In Petrakis's Power
Bought: For His Convenience or Pleasure?

Secret Heirs of Billionaires

The Sheikh's Secret Son

Seven Sexy Sins

A Taste of Sin

In Bed with the Boss

The Millionaire Boss's Baby
Secretary Mistress, Convenient Wife

Visit the Author Profile page
at Harlequin.com for more titles.

1

Maggie Cox

CLAIMING HIS PREGNANT INNOCENT

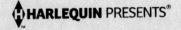

Recycling programs
for this product may
not exist in your area.

ISBN-13: 978-1-335-50445-6

Claiming His Pregnant Innocent

First North American publication 2018

Copyright © 2018 by Maggie Cox

This edition published by arrangement with Harlequin Books S.A.

For questions and comments about the quality of this book, please contact us at CustomerService@Harlequin.com.

Printed in U.S.A.

CHAPTER ONE

'WHAT DO YOU MEAN, the tenant wants more time to consider her position? Are you telling me she's refusing to vacate?'

Bastian Carrera couldn't believe what he'd just heard. It was the *last* thing he wanted to hear after spending the past month enthusiastically talking to buyers overseas in a bid to increase his family-owned company's market share of organic olive oil, and the day after tomorrow he would be out of the country again.

He'd returned home to Italy for a 'pit stop' before heading out to Brazil—not just on business, but to lecture. His family business was one of the leaders in its field, and many people were interested in how it had achieved its phenomenal success. The family might have the kind of personal wealth that most people could only dream of, and at thirty-six Bastian could have long ago taken things more easily if he'd wanted to, but he still took a personal interest in all aspects of the business.

However, the troubled expression on his father's bronzed, lined face now couldn't help but disturb him. It conveyed the guilt the older man plainly felt at not being able to give his son better news.

Just before Bastian had left he'd given notice to his tenants to quit the stone-built cottages they rented so they could begin work on the remaining acreage and get the rest of their land certified as organic. It generally took around three years to have the land converted, and his intention was to plant more groves with the finest organic olive trees.

For generations his family had established itself as one of the best olive oil producers in Italy and it had made their fortune, but it had never been just about making money. Their aim was to provide people with the very best produce they could deliver, and to that end Bastian took every chance he could to make improvements.

His father sighed. 'No… She is not exactly refusing, but—'

'Did you make it clear that she hasn't a

choice about whether she goes or stays? That we need the land for conversion?'

Reddening a little, Alberto Carrera shifted one shoulder. 'I did. But the lady doesn't want to go. She has not so long ago got divorced and is hoping to reignite her career. The light in the *villeta* is perfect for her work, she says, and she has set up her easel under the skylight.'

'And who is she…? A student of one of the great masters?' Unsympathetic, his son scowled.

'She is not that kind of artist. Lily is an illustrator of children's books and she says it is her right to remain in the *villeta* since she has signed a lease for two years and so far has only been renting for six months.'

The younger man scowled again and let loose a colourful curse. But, whatever emotion his expression might suggest, his visage was compelling—strong-boned and handsome as sin. Alberto proudly told people that his son's looks came from his mother's side…that all her family had been exceptionally beautiful. His only son was his last link to Annalisa, the enchanting girl he had fallen head over heels in love with all those years ago and lost far too soon when she'd died giving birth…

'And did you offer this woman the compensation we discussed and tell her we would find her somewhere equally suitable?'

'Yes, I did, son. But my sense is that she is not going to be so easily persuaded—and I can't blame her.'

Impatient now, Bastian dropped his hands to his hips, his dark eyes flashing, 'What do you mean, you can't blame her? You sound as though this woman has put you under some kind of spell, Father! I have just two days before business takes me abroad again and I need to know the land conversion is in hand before I go. Never mind… I will go and speak to her myself.'

As he descended the grand stucco steps of the family's house he was glad to get some air. His heart was pounding with indignant fury at this woman who imagined she could bend his father's will to suit her own. How *dare* she try and take advantage of him when Bastian wasn't around, perhaps seeing an opportunity to wear him down? He would soon set her straight…

On his way to the comparatively modest

stone cottage that his ancestors had built, he reflected some more on its stubborn occupant.

Not that he knew her or had even laid eyes on her. He left that part of the business to his father.

Alberto had become a little less able since his heart attack a year ago, and Bastian wanted him to keep his duties to a minimum. Along with the family's housekeeper, Dolores, they had a loyal workforce who tended the land and oversaw the olive growing, and Bastian himself quite often helped out because he loved being close to the earth. In his opinion, its scent was like no other...

His father hadn't complained too much about his new duties, thank God, and his son guessed he was only too aware that age was catching up with him. He'd practically worked himself into the ground, helping to build up the business, and the heart attack had quite rightly scared him...

Reaching the house that was set back from the olive groves, and gave its occupants plenty of privacy if privacy was what they sought, he negotiated the narrow stone steps with his usual agility. As he glanced up at one of the two wrought-iron balconies set beneath the sloping roof, with its plethora of red bougain-villea spilling through the decorative bars, he took a moment to breathe in the fragrance that saturated the air.

His tension started to ease. It was good to be home again, even if it wasn't for very long.

Quickly he remembered his reason for vis-iting and rapped commandingly on the door. In his view it was important that he imme-diately gained the upper hand with his re-calcitrant tenant and did not give her any advantage. At least that was the plan.

But the door opened suddenly and his gaze fell on a green-eyed fair-haired beauty who stood before him, barefoot and tousle-haired, in a sleeveless multi-coloured striped dress that couldn't help but pay homage to a body so slender she might have been a prima bal-lerina. All his plans flew out the window...

'Can I help you?' she asked, her pretty, un-adorned mouth clearly unsure as to whether to smile or not.

Where do I start? he thought. The shock-ing waves of potent want and need that swept through him powerfully just then all but stopped him from speaking. It was like

being scorched inside and out, and he feared
burning in the flames...

Hurriedly collecting himself, he replied,
'Signora Alexander? I am Bastian Carerra...
your landlord.'

'You mean you're Alberto's son?'

Now her lips *did* shape a smile. Was there a
woman alive who was immune to his father's
charm? Bastian mused. He could hardly believe this woman had been married and divorced, though. There was a real 'untouched'
air about her...

'That's right. Can I come in? I'd like a word
with you.'

Despite the heat of the day, he knew his
tone was a little frosty. No matter how attractive Lily Alexander was, he'd make no
bones about demanding she leave. After all,
business was business, and he wouldn't let
the demands of his libido override his common sense...

'We'll go into the sitting room. We can talk
there,' she suggested. 'But first of all can I
get you a drink?'

'No. I'd prefer it if we just talked.'

As she led this somewhat serious Italian
into the charmingly homespun living room,

with its very agreeable little balcony outside the French doors and in the distance a superlative view of the sea, Lily's heartbeat skipped a little.

The younger Carerra might appear somewhat humourless, but no one could deny he was hot… With his mussed dark hair touching his shoulders, prominent cheekbones and those sultry brown eyes that could make *any* woman melt if he looked at them directly, he certainly stirred the senses. And it didn't hurt that he wore his white cambric shirt and light blue jeans in an easy way that suggested he never had to worry about what he wore… That fit, toned body of his guaranteed that he'd look good in just about *anything.*

Catching herself, she realised it had been a very long time since she'd looked at a man with anywhere *near* longing. Life with a husband who hadn't been interested in intimacy had seen to that. In any case, she wouldn't let this pointless impulse to get to know the handsome Italian detract from her goal to continue renting the *villeta.* Coming here had given her the freedom she needed to concentrate on her work and earn a better living.

She'd always thought herself blessed to

have artistic skills, even if it had bemused her logically minded ex-husband.

'I can't pretend I understand your devotion to this drawing you do when you could easily have a much better-paid career if you put your mind to it,' he'd declared.

The problem was, Marc put all his energy into working as a broker in the City, and to him *money* was the only thing worth having. Lily should have known from the start that his values were a million miles away from hers. But her search for more stability in her life and her decision to marry a man with money and property, who could provide her with security, had led her completely astray.

Yes, Marc was attractive, engaging and witty, and when they'd first dated he'd regularly told her how much he enjoyed being with her, that he liked her better than any other woman he'd dated. What was not to like? But her feelings of friendship towards him had sadly not blossomed into desire.

On that subject, she'd become doubtful that she even had it in her to feel such an emotion.

In truth, what had started out as an enjoyable friendship categorically should never have led to marriage. That much was clear.

Shortly after they were married their relationship had very quickly lost its way. Added to that, Lily had quickly grown to despise the phoney London life they'd lived, because she hadn't been able to relate to his friends and colleagues who, in her opinion, put money and possessions over everything that was natural and good.

It hadn't been the life she would have chosen if she'd utilised some common sense and their divorce had been both inevitable and welcome. When she'd received her Decree Absolute a year ago she had determined never to do anything so foolish again as to marry someone she barely even knew. No, she would be much more sensible.

Knowing she could earn money from her craft was the one advantage she had in her favour. Along with her savings, it meant that she wouldn't have to depend on alimony. Yet Marc had still insisted she accept a generous cheque from him in order to help her get started in her new life. His reason for doing so was that he wanted them to remain friends and part amicably.

The charmingly aged Italian *villeta* she'd found provided her with just the surroundings she'd been looking for. It was the perfect place for her to work on her book illustrations and hopefully restore some confidence in herself. Particularly after a marriage that had made her doubt she would ever find a man who would truly desire her, or she him.

Perhaps she just didn't have what it took for that?

'Why don't we sit down?' she suggested, indicating the somewhat battered wine-coloured sofa while electing to sit in the chintz-covered armchair herself.

As Bastian settled himself Lily noticed that his hands rested on his knees, as though he might easily spring into action should the need arise. That surely suggested a man who found it hard to contain his energy and relax. Already sensing that he wanted to get their business over and done with as soon as possible, she hoped his impatience wouldn't steer her towards trying to ameliorate him.

'You remember a few weeks ago we gave you notice to vacate the property?' he began.

Her smooth brow furrowed. 'Yes. I was told that you needed the land for planting.'

'Well, I understand from my father that you've changed your mind about leaving?'

'I didn't agree with the request in the first place and I told him so. When I rented this place I signed a legal document that stated the period of rental was two years. So far I've only been here six months'

'I'm well aware of that, *signora*, but I hoped that our offer of financial compensation would take care of any inconvenience caused—as well as our promise to find you somewhere equally suitable for your requirements.'

Releasing a sigh, she sat up a little straighter. 'It's not just about practical considerations. I've—I've grown to love this place. Being here has helped me find the inspiration I was looking for.'

Lifting an enquiring dark brow, Bastian folded his arms. 'You have had trouble finding it elsewhere?'

'I had what you might call a dry period. I made an unwise decision and life got rather difficult for me for a while. Consequently I lost faith in my ability.'

With a helpless shudder she caught hold of her hands to stop them trembling, but she knew her companion hadn't failed to miss their slight quiver.

Why had she been so candid with him? She should learn to think before she spoke! Now he would probably suspect she wasn't entirely confident about their upcoming chat and that perhaps she was unsure as to where she stood regarding the legalities of her rental.

His deep brown eyes unsettled her with their frank intensity.

'But presumably your publishers still want your work?'

'Yes, they do. I illustrate the stories of a well-known children's writer, and so far I haven't had any complaints. The books are doing very well in spite of my recent challenges.'

'You do not wish to write your own stories and illustrate them?'

Funny he should ask that. It was one of her long-held dreams.

Lily swallowed hard. The knowing smile that dimpled his bronzed cheek was disconcerting. Now she trembled for a different reason... If he worked for MI6 he could probably persuade any female perpetrator of crime to confess immediately.

It shook her to her core to think of what that effortlessly sexy smile of his could do to a woman...

'Yes, I do. I've already written a couple but… Well, it's not an easy profession to get into.'

'So better to stick with what you know? Is that what you're saying?'

Indignant heat flooded her. 'I'm not saying that at all. I just think it's best to deal with one thing at a time.'

'You don't believe in taking risks, then?'

'You came here to talk to me about my tenancy, Signor Carrera… Don't you think we'd better just get on with that?' Endeavouring to sound firm, she felt wary of him seeing her as potentially weak and taking advantage.

Allowing his gaze to roam leisurely over the disconcertingly lovely features before him, Bastian realised that something that should have been easy—that he dealt with as a matter of course in his business life—suddenly felt tiresomely difficult.

Mulling over what she might have meant when she'd confessed that her life had been rather difficult lately and things had made her lose faith in her ability, he quickly ran his mind through the gamut of possibilities. Had she been bereaved? Was she recovering from an accident or an illness? Or had she lost her money in one of those deplorable financial scams?

Then it dawned on him.

She'd been recently divorced, his father had said. No doubt her confidence had been shaken by her marriage not working out. It must have been harder still if she'd really *loved* the man...

Because the idea disturbed him more than it ought, he steered his thoughts back to the matter in hand and said firmly, 'Very well, then. We will talk business. Regrettably, my father and I need you to vacate the property as soon as possible, *signora*, and we will gladly compensate you in order for you to do that. As you have already been advised, we will even find you similar suitable accommodation in the area.'

Lily rubbed her hands up and down her bare arms as if she was feeling cold. His heart thudded at the thought of a very particular way of warming her. It had been a long time since he'd felt so attracted to a woman, and the fact that he did so now, with *this* woman, would turn out to be a major inconvenience should he succumb to it.

'Do you really expect me to agree to leave

just like that?' she demanded, tucking a long strand of hair turned golden by the sun behind her ear. 'I have rights too, you know.'

'Of course you do. That's why we have made you a very good offer to help you agree to go. You will not be out of pocket, or left to find alternative accommodation on your own.' Taking a deep breath in, Bastian felt oddly ill at ease as he garnered himself to say what he had to say next. 'If you do not agree to leave, I'm afraid we may have to resort to having the authorities evict you.'

Immediately she pushed to her feet. Bastian saw her upper lip quiver and a vivid rose tint spread over her cheeks.

It made him feel like an absolute louse that he'd put her in such an untenable position. Never before had the necessity to do such a thing in the name of business overly disturbed him. From early on in his career he'd learned that he couldn't please everyone, that sometimes it was necessary to stick to his guns in order to get what he wanted. But it perturbed him that he was going to disappoint *her*.

'You would really do that? Do you honestly think that's fair?'

Lifting a broad, hard-muscled shoulder and

dropping it again, he aimed to keep his tone matter-of-fact and not resort to getting into a disagreeable confrontation. He was well aware that on rare occasions heightened emotions could get the better of him.

'We gave you plenty of notice.' Standing up, he drove his hand exasperatedly through his hair. 'Surely that was enough?'

'It wasn't…it *isn't*.'

Determined to let him know she was no pushover, Lily stood her ground. Bastian Carrera wasn't going to treat her as though she was some meek little lamb whose needs weren't important and get away with it! Other people had treated her in such a cavalier fashion before and she wouldn't tolerate it.

Memories came of being mocked at school for being shy and awkward and refusing to be part of any clique—it had singled her out to the class bullies. Their cruel taunts and efforts to exclude her from school activities had made her feel even more isolated and alone than she'd already felt at home. Hers had not been a loving household. But the pain of what she'd endured then made her even more determined to stand up to her landlord now.

'How would *you* like to be ousted from

your place of residence as though you don't matter? As if your needs are inconsequential?' Her tone rang with temper. 'People like me clearly don't matter to you so long as you get what you want, do they?'

'What do you mean by that?'

'You know very well what I mean. It's obvious you believe my needs are nowhere *near* as important as your own. I'm just an ordinary woman, trying to make her living in the best way I can, and I won't be dictated to by a man who thinks he's superior just because he's inherited wealth and land and doesn't have to depend on anyone for the fundamental things in life…like a *home*!'

'You think I don't appreciate what I have? That I take my good fortune for granted?' Bastian's glance was steely. 'You have no idea how wrong you are. I work as hard as—if not harder than—any of my employees who need to put food on the table for their families because that's what I learned from my father. His example taught me that a business is only as good as the people who run it—that we have to value those who work for us and let them know their contribution is essential to the success and wellbeing of us all.'

The passion in his voice made Lily realise how much her comment had got to him. She knew she'd sounded accusing and jealous of his good fortune and she hadn't meant to convey that at all. That wasn't the way she felt. All she wanted was to be treated fairly and not to be pushed aside like some annoying inconvenience.

'I didn't say that you took anything for granted. I take pride in working hard myself. It's just that...'

Disturbingly, she somehow found herself face to face with him, and she tried hard not to be distracted by his arresting presence for long enough to finish speaking her mind and let him know how furious she was at what appeared to be his distinct lack of understanding in her case.

'Couldn't this necessity of yours to turn over the land to more organic olive groves wait a while longer? At least until the agreed length of my tenancy expires? Can't you at least think about it?'

Breathing hard, she felt the uncomfortable sensation of sticky perspiration breaking out on her skin, making her feel damp. It was a particularly hot day, but the external temperature wasn't the only reason for the enervating heat that had descended on her…

It was Bastian Carrera himself.

When he didn't immediately reply she added lamely, 'Honestly…you make me so angry'

His smile was wry—taunting, almost. The fury he'd displayed just now had suddenly dissipated. Yet the residue of that heightened emotion seemed to be unaccountably turning into something far more threatening.

When she glanced back into those haunting, dark eyes of his she saw they were unapologetically sensuous.

'That is just the kind of thing a lover would say.'

'What are you talking about?'

She was too flustered to understand how or why events had taken a sudden one-hundred-and-eighty-degree turn, but they had. However, deep inside she *did* know.

The tangible tension between them that was now electrifyingly real had simply had to find an outlet.

As if to confirm it, the Italian's warm, slightly callused hand was suddenly on the back of her neck as he brought his face down to hers. There was no time to think about anything other than the urgent feelings that shockingly made her ache to know him in the most intimate way, to touch and explore him and see if he echoed her hunger.

When his lips voraciously descended on hers, to all but devour them, Lily had her answer. The uncontainable passion he expressed made her heart pound and her blood thicken with the viscosity of molasses. And, whilst her trembling hands held on to the banks of his shoulders as if they would never let go, he murmured something in husky-voiced Italian and slid his hot silken tongue into her mouth.

She groaned with pleasure. As the kiss became even more erotic it was as if the combustible route they were on was only going to lead to one destination...

As their insatiable contact deepened and grew hotter Lily's knees gave way, and the short sharp breaths she released against his mouth sounded almost agonised.

Bastian instinctively caught her round the waist to stop her from falling and effortlessly lifted her into his arms. Then he turned and carefully lowered her onto the sofa. Lily's heart beat like a war drum inside her chest.

But it didn't make her question the wisdom of what she was doing. Her senses were so captivated by the tantalising aroma of him, how he smelled and how he felt, that she knew it was already too late to turn back.

She was hypnotised beyond recall.

With held breath, she watched him hurriedly strip off his shirt. Before he came back to her she had a tantalising glimpse of sleek, tanned musculature that was everything a woman would dream of in a man. His silken toned biceps were like steel ropes beneath his skin, and he had a dusting of inviting ebony hair on his chest. With his deeply assessing brown eyes and a charisma second to none, Lily already knew he was impossible to resist.

Delving into the back pocket of his jeans, she saw him take out something and unzip his fly. In a wave of mercurial heat she realised he was going to protect himself. It shocked her that she hadn't thought of the need to do the same—but then she was scarcely familiar with such a necessity, was she?

As he positioned himself astride her, his weight pressed her down into the sofa. She heard the leather crackle and settle. Staring up, she knew her gaze was helplessly fixed on him.

Even the simplest of words were hard to summon right then. All thought and sense of time was suspended. Bastian was nipping at her mouth and kissing her forehead, cheeks and eyelids in turn, before pushing her dress up to her middle and caressing her slim torso. His mouth captured hers in a commanding sexy kiss and she felt his hands tug her dress up even higher. When he expertly undid her cream-coloured bra to release her small pert breasts, she gasped.

The sultry air that played against her bare skin had an immediate effect on her. It made her feel like a whole other woman.

Never in her life had Lily behaved so wantonly. But she had always known it would take a very special man to free her desires— a man who would give credence to his senses and wouldn't be afraid to express them.

Just a second later the Italian lowered his head to take a burgeoning nipple inside his mouth. When he grazed his teeth against her tender skin Lily moaned low and drove her hands into his hair to hold him there. It was the most erotic combination of pleasure and pain she'd ever experienced and she didn't want it to end.

He lifted his head and a lock of hair fell across his forehead. Meeting her aroused gaze, he spoke with a gravelly husk as he asked, '*Signora*, will you let me take you?'

Her answer was an unequivocal whispered, '*Yes...oh, yes...*'

Reaching down to her panties, he eased them down over her hips and discarded them. Laying his hands against her silken thighs, he pressed them apart. In less than a heartbeat he'd eased himself deep inside her.

A sharp pain made her wince momentarily and catch her breath, but the discomfort very quickly subsided. It was as if she'd been waiting for him all her life. He was hard and hot and everything she'd wanted and yearned for but hadn't known just how much until the very moment he claimed her.

Both the revelation and the visceral nature of the experience stunned her.

Bastian, too, was taken aback. His gaze was resting on her as though he couldn't quite believe what was happening.

'*Sei incredibile,*' he murmured.

No more was said as their bodies started to

move in the timeless motion that lovers the world over intuitively knew, and Lily instinctively wrapped her slender legs round his lean taut middle the better to accommodate him.

There was no thought of regret whatsoever.

How could she possibly regret something as amazing and sublime as this?

He had said she was incredible, but she would say the same about him—and more.

Never before had Bastian felt so turned on or so sexually hungry, as if he would go out of his mind if he didn't have her. Recalling that he'd mocked his father when he'd asked if Lily had put him under a spell, he now knew she had done exactly that to *him*.

She was utterly exquisite, with her silky soft skin, her long-lashed green eyes and hot, tight centre, and he hadn't missed the fact that she'd been a little *too* tight when he'd first taken possession. It had surprised him. Maybe the sexual intimacy between her and her ex hadn't worked out?

But all that was forgotten as he sensed her come undone. The muscles in his arms bunched harder as he held himself still, pausing to give her time to enjoy the release. It appeared as though she was utterly overwhelmed by the experience—as if she'd never encountered a similar response with a man before.

Bastian couldn't deny that the idea filled him with a surge of undeniable male pride. He was still entranced by the seductive sounds she'd made as he'd pleasured her, and this couldn't help but heighten his desire. But any further thoughts vanished as the very palpable need in him to attain his own culmination grew undeniably urgent.

'Look at me,' he commanded.

Lily complied, her green eyes shimmering like crystal, her beautiful golden hair spread out on the cushions behind her. He thrust hard as his craving grew ever more demanding, and when it reached its crescendo she held him as he cried out.

Gasping to get his breath, he fell against her. He could honestly attest that he had never had such mind-blowing sex with a woman before. They seemed to have the most inexplicable connection despite having only just met.

When he raised his head again, to study her face, he was shocked to find that her eyes were swimming with tears. What did that mean?

Carefully disengaging himself, he deftly

changed places wth her and pulled her firmly into his arms. In the aftermath of this extraordinary and unexpected spontaneous event his heart was racing as it had never raced before.

Concerned, he gently asked, 'Why do you cry, *mia dolce?* Did I hurt you?'

'No, you didn't. I don't know why I'm crying.'

Her soft whisper was as delicate as gossamer, and surprisingly she touched her hand to his cheek. Unable to resist taking it captive, he turned over the slender palm and touched his lips to her skin as though it was something infinitely precious.

What was the matter with him? He was behaving as though he had little control over his actions and that *had* to cause alarm. Lily's fire had burned him more than he'd thought possible…

CHAPTER TWO

'YOU HAVE TO LEAVE.'

His lover's voice was suddenly unequivocally firm. Even as she spoke Lily was getting to her feet, tidying her disarrayed hair
and straightening her dishevelled clothing.
She even reached down inside her dress to
pull out the bra he'd undone and despatched
it into a pocket.

It was hard to deal with the knowledge of
her being naked under the cheerful striped
dress without wanting her all over again. Bastian knew a powerful urge to insist she came
back to him and continued what they'd started
to his satisfaction. But he knew he didn't dare
do any such thing. It would be like pouring
fuel on a fire that already threatened to get
out of control.

If nothing else he needed time to take
stock, time to...

Rising to his feet, he dealt with the condom. Then he zipped up his jeans and snatched up his cambric shirt from the floor. Quickly pulling it on, he dragged his hand through his hair and turned to survey his companion.

'We haven't finished discussing your tenancy,' he declared, uneasy with the subject because of what had just occurred.

'You think I've forgotten that you want me out?' she answered testily.

'No. I didn't mean that.' Deliberately, he softened his tone. It was impossible to stay angry and frustrated with her when the woman had just taken him to heaven and back.

'But you still want me to vacate earlier than I should and—and—' Visibly squaring her shoulders, she stared back at him. 'Like I said, I have rights, and I'll explore just what they are with a solicitor if I have to. You're not going to get rid of me quite so easily, *signor.*'

Of all the things she might have said, he'd never expected that. In truth, he had to admit that he admired her for taking such a stance.

'Look, all I want to say is that I'm willing to come at things differently and give you a bit more leeway in the matter.'

'What?'

Knowing he had stupidly let his guard down, after being careful about his dealings with women for so long, Bastian felt he had no one to blame for this awkward situation but himself.

Rubbing his hand round his jaw, he told her, 'I mean you don't have to leave straight away. I've been unexpectedly invited to go to Brazil on business, and I anticipate I'll be gone for at least six weeks. In light of that, I've decided you can stay here until I return. When I get back we can review the situation. Is that more agreeable to you?'

'I won't deny having a bit more time to think about things and make some plans would be better.'

'Good. Then the matter is settled.'

'What about planting the new olive groves?'

'That, too, can be postponed until I get back.'

'I see…'

His beautiful tenant was stroking her hands up and down her arms as if they were chilled but, having just become personally acquainted with her warm embrace, he could attest to them being anything but cold when she'd wrapped them around him.

'Did what happened between us just now cause you to change your mind, Signor Carrera?'

'You can at least call me Bastian.'

On hearing his invitation, Lily immediately coloured. She knew that their being on first-name terms wasn't going to make their situation any simpler.

'Because if that's the case I don't want you feeling like you owe me anything.'

'Having met you, I do not in any way imagine you are the kind of woman who would be as easily placated as that.' Sighing, he unconsciously laid his hand over his heart in the now crumpled cambric shirt. 'In any case, I like to think I'm a reasonable man. If I didn't give your situation proper consideration after the intimacy we've just shared, and heartlessly demanded you leave right away, I would be letting *myself* down as well as you.'

'Well… I'm glad you feel like that.'

'But, whatever happens, don't think I regret what took place between us because I don't.'

In response, as if suddenly an intruding bright light had been trained on her, Lily's green eyes flashed. 'That's as may be, but it won't be happening again, *signor*. I can assure you of *that*!'

The comment made him smile. He walked to the door, and just before his hand alighted on the handle to open it he turned back, drawling lazily, 'We will have to wait and see about that, *signora,*' as if the matter was entirely open to debate...

Although determined not to dwell overlong on the fact that she'd just had the most incredible sex with a stranger, Lily knew it would be easier said than done. The unforeseen event had been completely out of character for her, and it was hard to believe it had happened.

She'd taken a huge risk in not thinking of protecting herself. Thank goodness her lover had used a condom. He'd obviously been prepared for such a situation, while *she* was so inexperienced it was laughable...

Still, in the shower she mentally revisited the excitement and pleasure Bastian had given her and gently touched all the places he'd helped to make tender. Combing out her hair in front of the antique mirror in the bedroom, she carefully scrutinised her reflection. She even *looked* like a different person, she decided. Somehow she seemed to have acquired the rosy cheeks and wide-eyed expression of a veritable *ingénue*.

Still a little dazed, she returned to her drawing board under the skylight. It would hardly help her, being so distracted, and the tingling in her body and the long-buried ache the Italian had stirred into life again would inevitably tax her concentration.

But at least she didn't have to leave the *villeta* straight away. Her landlord's decision to let her stay a little while longer gave her some much-needed breathing space in which to mull over her predicament and make some decisions.

During the next few days, as well as undertaking her paid work, Lily started to set aside regular time for her own stories and drawings. Unbeknownst to him, the handsome Italian had issued her with a challenge when he'd asked why she didn't want to write and illustrate stories herself. The more she thought about it, the more she decided she would seriously consider the idea. Even if it didn't work out, she ought to at least give it a try.

Lily reminded herself that it was her ex who had thought she was wasting her time doing her drawing when she could have a much better paid career. Bastian didn't think that that way. Maybe her handsome landlord had unknowingly suggested the very thing she needed to hear?

For the first few days after he had departed for Brazil, Lily often asked herself why she had behaved so wantonly…as if she had no morals at all? But, recalling how it had been between her and the Italian—the instant connection, the impossible-to-resist sexual hunger their meeting had aroused—how could she regret it? More to the point, how would she handle the temptation of him when he returned? Could she risk having sex with him again without any consequences, even though she'd insisted that she wouldn't?

In light of that, she thought that maybe she should arrange to put some more distance between them and move into the other house they'd offered her before he got back after all? Sighing, she decided to talk to his father Alberto about it. She'd become rather fond of the older man, and instinctively knew he would give her some good advice.

But four weeks after his son had left the country, Lily's period was late. And after taking the pregnancy test she'd bought from the local *farmacia* in a bid to reassure herself, she made the startling discovery that she was pregnant…

July, August and September were winter months in Brazil, but the temperatures were similar to that of an Abruzzo summer. Being acclimatised to the heat, Bastian barely noticed it. Much more prevalent in his mind was the volatile situation he'd left behind him.

He was well used to women coming on to him, but that hadn't been the case with his beautiful young tenant. Instead they had become shockingly intimate practically on sight. It was as though some greater power had been driving them that day—a power that they had responded to straight away and hadn't even questioned. Any concept of right or wrong hadn't entered their minds.

Maybe it was precisely the fact that Lily hadn't pursued him in the way he was used to that was the reason he couldn't put the stunning woman from his mind. Like it or not, his business with Lily was far from concluded, and he found himself counting the days until they could be reunited.

And this time things would be brought to a close between them—one way or another!

Lily had been busier than usual. Since she'd found out that she was pregnant she'd not only attended to her illustrations and worked diligently on her own children's stories, she'd also started to make her new accommodation much more homely.

The new house was more spacious than the *villeta* had been, and just as beautifully appointed. To bring a touch of her own personality she'd draped the generous-sized couch and armchairs with silk shawls and the plumped-up cushions that she'd bought from a local market in the town. She also made sure that the large burnt orange ceramic bowl that she'd found in the kitchen was always filled with plenty of fruit.

It would help to remind her that she had to eat especially well now, due to the baby.

But what was done was done. She'd been responsible for protecting herself but she hadn't, and this was the consequence.

She'd never properly contemplated the

monumental change a child would bring into her life and the prospect was undeniably scary. Some would say her decision to have the baby as a single woman was an irresponsible one. But the idea excited her. Life suddenly seemed to take on much more meaning.

The challenge of writing her own stories as well as illustrating other authors' work to help pay the rent had grown to encompass the unexpected miracle that was taking place inside her body. In truth, Lily was excited at the prospect of taking care of the child and raising him or her.

The only fly in the ointment was that she hadn't shared her news with Bastian yet. He was still away. When he found out about it would he think she expected him to support her and the baby? The thought made her shudder. It had undoubtedly come as a shock to discover she was pregnant, but it was *her* decision to go through with it.

There was no way she wanted to be beholden to another man—especially after the mistake she'd made in marrying her husband. But sooner or later her handsome landlord would be home and, like it or not, she would have to tell him everything.

In the meantime, although she missed the *villeta* with its inspiring skylight and the vista of olive groves, the traditional stone house she was now renting from the Carreras was just as appealing. For one thing it was closer to the sea, and yet it was surrounded by the most idyllic countryside. Another plus was that every morning she woke to the sound of the waves lapping on the shore, and towards evening witnessed some of the most dramatic sunsets she'd ever seen.

As for Alberto's advice about moving there when she'd gone to see him, he had been kindness itself.

'You must do what your heart tells you to do, *signora*,' he'd said. 'Despite what my son may have told you, there is no need for you to panic about the situation. We can wait for you to decide. Whether you choose to leave the *villeta* in the time suggested or to move into one of our other houses, first and foremost we want you to be happy. We have not always been so fortunate as to have tenants as reliable and charming as you, Lily.'

He'd clasped her to his chest and kissed her soundly on both cheeks. She'd grown very fond of the man, and loved the way his brown eyes crinkled at the corners and sparkled when he was pleased about something. The warmth he conveyed was undoubtedly reassuring.

She wondered if Bastian shared his father's quality to soothe and reassure...

He was agitatedly pacing up and down, his boot-heels making the dust motes fly up from the floorboards. Meanwhile his father sat upright in his favourite kitchen chair and patiently allowed his son to vent.

'I cannot *believe* you let her move out just like that!' Bastian fumed. 'As I understood it she was going to say at the *villeta* until I returned from my trip. Plus, she said working under the skylight there helped inspire her to do her best drawing. What if that doesn't come so easily to her in the new house?'

The younger Carrera came to a sudden standstill, dropped his hands to his denim-clad hips and glared.

'Why are you suddenly so concerned as to whether the *signora*'s surroundings inspire her or not? You certainly weren't before. We both know the *villeta* has to be demolished in order to convert the land. Isn't that what you urged me to remember when you thought I was being too soft with her? I thought you wanted her to leave as soon as possible?'

'I did… I *do*.'

Feeling ill at ease, Bastian impatiently pushed back the rebellious lock of hair that tumbled onto his brow. What *was* it about this woman that drove him to such levels of agitation? Again he recalled that feeling that she had bewitched him.

'Forget what I said. If she is quite happy with the arrangement then that suits all of us, does it not? I will call in to see her later, to see how she's settling in. And to thank her for co-operating at last!'

Releasing a sigh that sounded as if he'd been holding it in for ever, he crossed the floor to squeeze the other man's shoulder affectionately. Narrowing his gaze, he examined him searchingly.

'Have you been okay? Dolores tells me that she's been making sure you've been eating well and are getting as much rest as possible. I trust that there's been no more chest pain or anything like that?'

Alberto scowled. 'Between the two of you, you make me feel like a sick child who needs round-the-clock care! Now, instead of fussing over me, why don't you sit down and tell me all about your trip to Brazil. Was it worthwhile?'

His son grinned. 'Need you ask? You should know by now that I never embark on a business trip that isn't fruitful!'

CHAPTER THREE

It HAD BEEN a long time since Bastian had been up this way to look at their properties. And even though he knew their caretaker Mario made sure that everything was kept in tip-top condition, Bastian was surprised to see how homely this particular rental house looked.

It was built in the style of a traditional Italian farmhouse, and inside the old-fashioned brick ceilings had been restored and a tasteful degree of modernity added. The kitchen, bedrooms and bathrooms were particularly spacious, and the sea views spectacular.

Outside, at the front of the house, he could see that the earth in between the concrete slabs they'd had laid looked to be recently dug over, ready for planting. Already some bulbs had been bedded in and had started to sprout. There were tantalising glimpses of pink, blue and yellow blooms. Most of the frontage had been pragmatically concreted into a patio… they hadn't had flowerbeds there for a long time.

Was Lily responsible for this very satisfying new arrangement? He knew Mario would never have taken it upon himself to do such a thing without discussing it with him first…

Rubbing a hand round his jaw, Bastian was still mulling over the changes as he nimbly negotiated the steps to the front door and was surprised to find it open. With a brisk knock against the wood panelling, he put his head round the door.

'Anybody home?' he called out, first in his native Italian and then in English.

'Is that you, Alberto? Just give me a minute, will you? I'm in the middle of something…'

At the sound of the voice he hadn't realised quite how much he'd been longing to hear, he stepped inside. His pretty tenant was seated with her back to him at the rustic chestnut desk he'd installed long ago, her pencil deftly moving across a large sheet of paper on a drawing board, clearly intent on concentrating.

Her sunlit hair was scooped up behind her

head with a simply knotted scarf fashioned out of some emerald-green gauze, and it exposed the lovely ballerina-like slope of her neck. He stilled for a moment, aching to touch his lips to that flawless and inviting bare skin. Thankfully he controlled the impulse just in time, because Lily suddenly turned round and saw him.

Immediately colouring, she said, 'Signor Carrera... I didn't know you were back from your trip. When did you return?'

Dropping her pencil onto her sketch pad, she got to her feet, unconsciously smoothing her hand over her hair. Today she was wearing a sleeveless white top that exposed her delicately tanned slim arms, teamed with apricot silk palazzo pants that rippled like the gentlest of streams when she moved.

Bastian tried doubly hard to keep his desire at bay.

'Yesterday...in the early hours of the morning.'

'Then no doubt you must still be feeling quite tired?'

'Not at all...the thought of coming home always helps revitalise me.'

'Well, I...' Flushing a little, she gestured

towards the kitchen. 'Can I get you a drink of something?'

'No. There's nothing I want right now.' *Except you,* his mind flashed. 'How do you like your new accommodation?'

'I love it. I don't know why I worried so much about moving.'

'Good—that pleases me. I can see that you're working. Mind if I take a look?'

'Be my guest. It's an illustration I'm doing for a new book.'

As she stood back to let him draw closer Bastian breathed in the intoxicating scent that indelibly clung to her. It reminded him of all the good things in life that he loved combined... How could he have forgotten it after the intimacy they had shared?

Even as his blood heated at the memory his gaze fell on the captivating sketch of a tortoiseshell cat with enormous green eyes and an exaggerated suggestion of determination on its face.

'Is this for someone else's story or one of your own?'

'Does it matter?'

'Yes, I think it does. It's very good, but I'd rather it was for one of yours.'

'Why?'

He folded his arms and looked at her...*really* looked at her...almost as if for the very first time. His examining gaze reunited him with the reality of her beauty and grace and, whilst he'd never been possessive about women before, the pleasure and satisfaction that coursed through his veins at knowing he'd made her *his*, couldn't be measured.

'Two reasons. First because it reminds me of *you*, and I'm guessing any stories you write must equal your drawing talent, and second because it's too good to give to someone else.'

Feeling undeniably self-conscious, she nodded. 'Well, you've guessed right. I took your advice and this is an illustration for one of my own stories.'

'So you have taken up your writing more seriously?'

'Let's say I'm *trying* to.'

'And what's this expression of determination on the cat's face about?' The corners of his mouth lifted in gentle amusement.

'You'll have to read the book to find out. That is if it's published.'

'Why wouldn't it be when, going by this

engaging illustration, you clearly know how to bring a children's story to life? What's the title?'

'If I had my way I'd like it to be called *There's No Such Word as Can't.*'

'Is that a piece of advice you were given growing up?'

With an awkward shrug of her slim shoulders Lily tried for a smile but didn't quite manage it.

'Yes…but I haven't always been able to apply it. My teacher once said it to me on a school trip to France, when I woke her up in the middle of the night because I couldn't sleep. I was afraid of the dark, you see. After telling me there was nothing to fear, and that soon I would be back home and wishing I'd enjoyed the trip more instead of worrying, she told me to go back to bed and try harder to get some sleep. That's when I said, *I can't.*'

'How old were you at the time, Lily?'

'About nine or ten.'

'Being away from home at that age would be bound to make most children anxious. I'm sure you weren't alone in feeling that.'

She frowned. 'The other girls in my room didn't seem to have a problem. The thing is…

I should have been braver. I felt like such an idiot.'

'You were no such thing,' Bastian said firmly. 'You were just a child. Anyway, I don't doubt your teacher's comment helped you because you remembered it. Perhaps you're more determined to overcome your fears now, yes?'

'I'd like to think so.'

'It seems to me that a lack of belief in yourself is what hurts you the most, Lily.'

'How do you know so much about me when we've only just met?'

Her near-whispered response was tentative. And even the air around them just then felt as if it was holding its breath, loaded as it was with a peculiar kind of danger that only *they* knew the reason for. Bastian was quite aware that the inevitable discussion that loomed was as potentially threatening as a hand grenade thrown into the room.

'Mind if I change my mind about that drink you offered?' he asked.

'Not at all—what would you like?'

'A cup of coffee would be good. Black, one sugar.'

'I'll see to it. Why don't you sit down?'

He elected to sit in the armchair, judging it to be safer than the couch after what had happened before. But his mouth was dry as sand as he waited for her to return with their drinks, and he still didn't know what he was going to say.

How could he explain the reason for what had seemed inevitable as soon their eyes had met?

Besides, Lily was not simply some pretty young woman he'd had an inconsequential tumble with that he could put down to experience and quickly forget. Their connection had gone way deeper than that, and as a consequence she had really got into his blood…

'Here you are. I hope I haven't made it too strong for you?'

Carrying both their drinks over to the generous-sized occasional table, his hostess turned one of the mugs towards him then sat down on the sofa.

'*Grazie.*' Smiling, he took a sip. '*Perfetto…* you have made it just how I like it.'

Sounding relieved, she murmured, 'I'm glad. So, how did your business trip go?'

She was just making small-talk, but she couldn't disguise her tension and Bastian easily detected it. Coming to a sudden decision, he returned his mug to the table. Then, drawing the back of his hand across his lips, he leant forward to meet her gaze candidly.

'We won't waste any more time talking about my trip. You and I both know we have to discuss what happened before I left,'

Of all the scenarios she'd imagined for when her charismatic landlord returned, Lily had not envisaged him being so blunt. As if to heighten her predicament, an unhelpful wave of nausea rolled through her just then. The strong scent of the herbal tea she'd made seemed to be making her feel queasy.

Returning the offending brew to the table, she sat back in her seat and folded her arms across her waist. She wasn't showing yet, but in a couple more months she would be. Her breasts already felt noticeably heavier.

Lifting her gaze, she carefully examined her companion. How could she have forgotten for even a second how handsome he was? With his curling dark hair, seductive long-lashed brown eyes and the fit, muscular body that was clearly no stranger to working the land, she could tell his occupation had helped to make him fit and strong. In another age he would have been in demand to sit for *any* of the great artists or sculptors, she was sure…

'I don't know quite what you're expecting me to say, Signor Carrera…'

There was a flash of amusement in his dark eyes at her formal address. 'So we're back on landlord and tenant terms, are we? I'm asking if you've had any further thoughts about what happened between us…or have you assumed we'll carry on as though nothing remotely out of the ordinary happened at all?'

Lily didn't have a prayer of behaving as if the memory didn't disturb her. She'd sensed the heat rise in her cheeks the instant she'd realised her unexpected caller wasn't Alberto but instead his compellingly attractive *son*. Many times she'd fantasised about what she would say when she saw him again, but now she was tongue-tied and awkward. Particularly because she yet had to tell him about the far-reaching consequences of their brief but unplanned afternoon of pleasure.

'I'm not saying we should act as if nothing happened. To tell you the truth, we *can't*.'

'What do you mean?'

Her insides were churning with crazy feelings of hope mingled with anxiety. Seeing

Bastian again, the last thing…the *very* last thing she could do was pretend indifference to the situation.

'Are you trying to tell me that there's someone else on the scene? Is that why you want to forget about what happened?'

The affront in his voice took her aback. Tucking a stray strand of pale gold hair back into her bun, from where it had drifted free, it wasn't easy to keep her hands from trembling.

'There isn't anyone else…and I can hardly forget what happened when—'

'When what?' He leant forward, his hands on his knees as if he were immediately ready to spring to his feet and confront anything he found remotely disagreeable.

Understandably nervous, her heart racing like a greyhound's as it came out of the trap, Lily lifted her head and bravely met the Italian's glowering stare.

This was no time to give way to fear, she told herself.

'When I find myself expecting your baby.'

CHAPTER FOUR

BASTIAN BROKE THE sudden silence that had fallen between them with a gravel-voiced reply. 'You're pregnant?'

He vacated his seat to come towards her and a carved muscle flinched ominously in the side of his unshaven cheek. Clearly affected by the news, he seemed shaken.

'I wouldn't joke about it.'

Her heart thumped even harder. Wasn't confession supposed to be good for the soul? Whoever had come up with *that* one clearly hadn't been thinking straight! This was without a doubt one of the most difficult situations she'd ever had to deal with. It was even more difficult than when she'd finally told her ex that she wanted to end their marriage, because he'd kept back a vital truth about himself and she'd found she could no longer live a lie.

'When did you find out you're pregnant?'

'Not too long after you left… I didn't get my period and I'm usually quite regular.'

'But you took a test? To make sure, I mean?'

Her visitor moved in closer and the sensual quality of his aftershave registered deep in the pit of Lily's stomach. She bit down hard on her lip. Was this to be her challenge? To stay strong in the face of wanting him so much when as soon as she saw him his presence rendered her immediately weak?

'Yes, I did. I bought a test from the local *farmacia*. But to tell you the truth it wasn't necessary. I know my body well enough to sense that there are some changes taking place.'

Driving his hands through his hair, Bastian looked to be thinking hard. Then he abruptly moved away. Folding his arms, he said with worrying calmness, 'Then there really is only one solution. You will have to marry me.'

'What? But that's crazy!'

'Why? Does it surprise you that I would want to do the right thing by you? Or perhaps you can't handle the idea of us having a more permanent relationship since your previous marriage obviously didn't end well?'

'How do you know that?'

'I'm guessing.'

Taken aback, Lily didn't trouble herself to go into an explanation. Dominating her mind was the Italian's assertion that she would have to marry him.

'Anyway, getting back to your so-called solution…it would be crazy for us to get married. We hardly know each other. You're my landlord and I'm your tenant. We don't have a personal relationship. All we have between us is…'

'Some hot, unplanned sex?' he finished for her, quirking his brow.

'Some unexpected intimacy, I was going to say.'

It was hard to stop herself from blushing like a schoolgirl. But, more to the point, she could hardly believe Bastian was willing to legalise their relationship because of the baby. It just didn't seem plausible. He was a wealthy landowner and she was… Well, she was nobody important.

'The main consideration in this situation, Lily, is the baby. Although we can't know as yet if we have anything else in common, at least we know we are compatible physically.

Given that, I think you should seriously consider the idea of becoming my wife.'

Her body flooded with indignation. 'Things don't have to be as cut and dried as that. The world is full of single mothers. And besides…'

'Go on?'

'I don't want anyone else to decide my fate.'

Pushing to her feet, she instinctively rested her hand against her belly, as if to protect herself and her precious cargo.

'I didn't expect you to suggest marriage. I take full responsibility for making my own decisions and I intend to support this child by myself…however hard it might be.'

'You'll be making your life even harder if you go down that route. In any case, I don't think managing things on your own is the best decision to make. The baby is mine too. Which brings me to my next question.'

His glance held hers, as if daring her to look anywhere else for even a second.

'Why didn't you consider an abortion when you discovered you were pregnant? A lot of women in your position might have.'

Lily was shocked. 'I know you don't really know me, but I already consider this baby to be my child. I already love it. And I very much wanted it—right from the beginning.'

'I am very glad to hear it.'

There was an undoubted suggestion of satisfaction in his tone that told her he was pleased with her answer.

He continued, 'But, while I know I have to consider what you want, Lily, I have to tell you that as the baby's father I fully intend to do my duty and support you both.'

'You don't have to do that. We're living in the twenty-first century—not the Middle Ages!'

Grimacing, Bastian was far from amused by the remark. 'You think it backward for a baby's father to want to look after its mother? In my view that's where society has gone wrong. It's *good* to define our roles and stand by them.'

'Why?' she snapped back. 'Do you even *want* to be a father?'

He stilled, piercing her with a steely glare. 'That's hardly the point. We will deal with what *is*. The fact is I intend to honour my responsibilities—not run away from them. Whether that has been your previous experience of the men in your life or not, it makes no difference to me. I will do what's right and take care of my family.'

If Lily was honest she *liked* the idea of him referring to her and the baby as his family, and she admired him for owning up to his responsibility even if it did unsettle her. But the idea of him wanting to stand by her and the baby and take care of them was the stuff dreams were made of, wasn't it?

The trouble was, previous experience had shown her that people rarely lived up to such promises.

Breathing out a sigh, she sat down again and reached for a padded velvet cushion to hold in front of her. 'Despite what you say, I think you really ought to take some more time to think about this. You've just come back from your trip, and you told me you were going to start converting the land when you returned. It's your family's livelihood, and I'm quite aware that that has to come first.'

Raising a lightly mocking eyebrow, he remarked, 'You really expect me to believe that *you* won't put your *own* needs first? I have to say that's not been my usual experience with women.'

She sensed her cheeks glowing with heat. Her blood was throbbing with a ridiculous sense of betrayal.

She didn't really want to know about his experiences with other women. Just the thought of his having his arms round someone else was anathema to her.

'Look, I told you I don't need your help and I meant it. Independence is important to me, and if marriage to my ex taught me anything it's that men will usually put themselves before any woman in their life.'

He was already shaking his head in disagreement. 'I'm sorry if that's been your experience. Most Italian men take great pride in taking care of their women and children. Family means everything to us.'

The mention of family brought to mind the loss of his mother and the impact it had had on him and his father. Although he hadn't ever known her, there wasn't a day that went by when he didn't think about how different his life might have been if he'd known her love and care...

And in all these years Alberto had been alone. He was the kindest, most loving man in the world, but he had lost the one woman

in his life who had meant *everything* to him.
He had never sought to replace her—because
how could you replace sheer perfection? he'd
asked his son.

Thinking about his own past failed relationships, and one in particular, Bastian was
fearful that he was destined to suffer similar heartbreak, because he couldn't bear the
thought of taking a wife only to lose her—
particularly in childbirth.

Thankfully, his feelings for Lily were nowhere near like the ones his parents had had
for each other. He wouldn't be risking his
heart when they married. He would take care
of her and adore their children—because undoubtedly there would more after this baby—
and he would be the best husband he could be.
But ultimately their union would be a marriage of convenience…with undisputed *ben-
efits*, he added wryly to himself.

'That must be a wonderful way to be,' his
companion murmured. 'I imagine Alberto was
an amazing dad when you were growing up?'

'He was.'

'But you must have been lonely sometimes
with just each other to talk to? I mean without—without your mother?'

'He told you about that, then?' Bastian was mindful of not displaying any emotion about this, and deliberately kept his tone level. He felt aggrieved that his father had shared such a personal matter with Lily when as far as he was aware she was to all intents and purposes just their tenant.

'It came out in a conversation we had.'

'Anyway…we weren't always alone,' he asserted firmly. 'I have two aunts who made sure we were looked after, and several cousins. My father also hired Dolores. We had plenty of company if we wanted it.'

Not completely buying that last sentence, and feeling inexplicably sad, Lily collected her disagreeable beverage and took the mug out into the kitchen. To her surprise, she sensed her visitor following her.

She rinsed the crockery under the tap, and it stunned her when he suddenly reached out and grasped her forearm. For a second the touch of his skin was like standing too close to a roaring fire. She could barely think straight, let alone talk…

Turning off the tap, and letting the mug clatter into the basin, she turned warily. 'What is it?'

'How did you and your ex-husband meet? I've been wondering.'

Her stomach plunged in surprise. 'We met at a dinner party a friend gave.' She knew she sounded reluctant to say more.

'Go on.'

'Well…this friend was always trying to match me up with men because she thought I was too reclusive. Anyway, Marc and I met and immediately liked one another. We had a few dates, and quite soon he asked me to marry him. My friend was convinced it was a good idea…that he ticked all the right boxes…and in her view it was much better than my being alone.'

'So that was your criteria?' Bastian sounded vaguely disparaging. 'Your friend thought he was a good bet and it would save you from being alone?'

'Don't get me wrong—I really did like him. He was charming, considerate and kind to me. But quite soon after we got together I started to see that maybe making such a serious commitment to him hadn't been one of my best ideas. For one thing, he worked as a broker in the City and we were just too different.'

'Explain.'

She huffed out a sigh. 'I'm a creative person, and money isn't the be-all and end-all to me like it was for him. Our values were miles apart. That's a pretty important difference, wouldn't you say? Anyway, we agreed to part. I decided that if I was lonely in the future I'd be much better off getting a pet rather than another man. They're far less troublesome.'

His lips curved helplessly. 'I disagree. You just chose the *wrong* man.'

'Hindsight is a wonderful thing, isn't it?'

Withdrawing her arm, she was glad to be free of his touch in order to breathe more easily. It was hard to feel in command of her faculties when he stood so near.

'In any case, I'll need some time to reflect on what you've said. Can we leave things as they are for now?'

Saying nothing, he abruptly moved back through the crafted stone and brick archway that led into the living room. Lily took her time following him. One thing he'd demonstrated was that he had an iron will and would aim to have his way in anything he deemed important. If she agreed to marry him she guessed she would always have to fight her corner…

'The next time we talk we'll discuss arrangements for the wedding. I know you're still unsure, but you don't have to waste any more time wondering if it's a good thing or not. I'm not looking for any kind of romantic relationship, so you'll have no worries on that score. Our union will be purely pragmatic. Given time, I'm certain you'll be glad to have my support rather than deal with the prospect of motherhood on your own. The last thing you need is to let any anxieties you have transfer themselves to the baby.'

'Of course I wouldn't want that. But wait a minute… I still haven't made up my mind. I already have one failed marriage behind me and I'm not exactly eager to repeat that mistake by going into another one.'

'Our marriage won't fail, Lily…not if we both go into it clearly knowing what we want.'

His reasoning startled her. 'And what *do* you want out of it, Bastian? You've already said you're not looking for romance.'

Beneath his bronzed skin his complexion reddened. 'It's better if we discuss this tomorrow. Right now I have to head back. I have a lot of work to get on with.'

'I have too, but I think we should at least clarify things before we part, don't you?'

Bastian stilled for a moment, his carefully assessing glance giving her the impression he was trying to make her out. It reminded Lily that they hardly knew each other at all. Yet somehow there was an undeniable bond between them that she couldn't explain and equally couldn't resist...

'I'm hardly eager to put myself in the shark's mouth again any time soon by getting tangled up in emotion,' he said seriously. 'But knowing we've both suffered disappointment and hurt in the past can help us. I mean that it can work to our advantage. If we don't invest our feelings in this marriage too much then it can be more like a business contract. If we agree on the terms then it will ensure we are both more likely to be satisfied.'

Lily swallowed hard. To be honest, she felt sick. To her mind it didn't sound appealing at all. She wouldn't and *couldn't* be satisfied with such a cold arrangement—even if it meant she would have support for her baby.

It still made her blood turn to ice when she remembered Marc's deception and her travesty of a wedding night.

'So, in effect, we're destined to be alone even if we live together as husband and wife?' she commented. 'I mean, not to have even the smallest bit of comfort from our union sounds like a rather cold bargain to me.'

'I'm not suggesting we won't be intimate. Some things are fundamental. Do you think I would deny us the opportunity of enjoying one of the most incredible comforts of all— that which brought us together in the first place? I confess I couldn't be with you and live without it.'

She knew her face must have immediately turned scarlet. Yet knowing she felt the same as he did terrified her—because how could she *not* engage her feelings if they were to make love regularly?

'Tomorrow evening,' he declared suddenly. 'Shall we say around eight?'

Dumbfounded, she stared as he headed straight to the front door.

He didn't look back at her even once.

Instead he let the door slam shut.

The discordant sound seemed to reverberate around her body, and she had the sense that she was standing on a precipice, wrestling with the decision whether to jump or simply to turn back and accept whatever came next...

Bastian had decided to walk to his dad's place rather than drive the car. Having been cooped up in boardrooms and planes for long enough, he needed to breathe in some fresh air. Now, on his way back to the olive groves, the most pertinent thing on his mind was the knowledge that he was going to be a father.

It hardly seemed real. Ever since he'd heard the news Bastian had felt as though he were in a dream. It had been one of his greatest desires to become a father eventually, but he had shelved the idea a long time ago, after his ex, Marissa, had so heartlessly cheated on him.

There was an aching loneliness inside him that had been there since he was small, when even his dad hadn't been able to fill the gap. He'd realised he was mourning his mother more and more, even though he hadn't known her, and the feeling had been made worse by sometimes hearing his strong father weeping sorrowfully at night, when he'd thought Bastian was asleep.

When he was a little boy, he'd once asked him, 'Do you still miss Mamma…what was she like?'

He'd never forgotten his father's reply.

'Your *mamma* was like one of God's own angels, my son. A more beautiful or kind woman never walked the earth, and I will never forget her. It is my greatest regret that she left this life too soon.'

Ever since Marissa had so badly let him down Bastian had kept his personal desires—the things he really longed for—scrupulously to himself. But one thing he'd always believed was that every child deserved parents who were trustworthy, loving and loyal, and he'd vowed that when he *did* marry it would be to a woman who unquestionably had all of those exemplary qualities and more…

A light breeze ruffled his hair as he walked, and now that the blossoms on the trees had faded the strong aroma of the olive groves drifted towards him. It not only gave him the greatest satisfaction that their produce had given him and his family so much, but he felt as if he was a custodian of what had once been one of the most symbolic plants of ancient Rome.

One day he would teach his children the history of the groves and the symbolism of the olive branches. In his mind's eye he was already seeing the features of his first child. He imagined that he or she would be a perfect blend of himself and their mother, and he would never forget that it was his and Lily's extraordinary passion that had given them this chance to bring another human being into the world and hopefully oversee a healthy and happy future for them.

Even if their union had been anything *but* planned…

By the time he reached his father's kitchen his nostrils had scented the aroma of one of his favourite pasta dishes cooking, and he saw the older man standing at the free-standing range cooker with their housekeeper, Dolores, laughing at something she'd said as she stirred the sauce.

Bastian had already decided he wouldn't tell him straight away that he was going to be a grandfather, but would save the news until after he and Lily had started to make their wedding plans. But he couldn't help his heart racing nineteen to the dozen in anticipation of his father's reaction when he heard the news.

'Got another serving for the favourite son?' he joked.

Her dark hair now generously peppered with grey, Dolores turned round fast, her brown eyes brimming with pleasure. In her early seventies now, she was still an attractive woman.

'As usual, you have perfect timing, *mi querido.* Of course there is another plate for you!'

'The boy needs his own woman to feed him,' Alberto grumbled playfully. 'Then he won't have to come home all the time to eat.'

'You would hate it if I didn't come home from time to time—you know you would. And when I marry I intend for my wife to also come and enjoy your food.'

His father's bushy eyebrows shot up into his hairline. 'Are you telling me that you've met someone?'

'I don't want to get your hopes up, Father. It's like I've always said—nothing will happen on that score until the time is right.'

The other man expelled an exasperated

breath. 'What does *that* mean? Do you always have to be so enigmatic?'

Unable to hold back his laughter, Bastian realised it felt good to connect with his parent on something other than work. It made him remember all the good times they'd shared when he was a child—how with just a teasing phrase or two and a gentle good humour his father would put right everything that was troubling him and restore some calm. Even when things had been strained, they'd always ended on a high note.

'You have only yourself to blame for that,' he responded cheerfully. 'You always taught me to keep my cards close to my chest, to keep people guessing.'

'What is that French word I'm looking for?' With an ironic smile Alberto thoughtfully stroked his beard. 'I have it…*touché.*'

Saying nothing, Dolores gave him one of her looks and decisively moved across to a generously filled cabinet and reached for some dinner plates. Then she turned round and said to the younger man, 'Instead of just standing there looking pretty, Bastian Carrera, why don't you help me to lay the table?'

Making a mock salute, Bastian grinned. 'But of course, *signora*. Who am I to argue with my elders?'

The housekeeper picked up a dishtowel and threw it at him.

CHAPTER FIVE

LILY HAD BEEN on tenterhooks all day, waiting for Bastian to arrive. Even applying herself to her illustrations hadn't helped to still her mind and drown out the racing thoughts that crowded in on her like an encroaching storm.

Finally giving up on her attempts to work, she'd busied herself with cleaning the house from top to bottom, even though it didn't need it. At least it would give her the satisfaction of knowing that Bastian would see that she cared about these things and didn't *always* have her head in the clouds, dreaming.

At a quarter to eight she ran into her bedroom to change out of the loose cotton shirt and jeans she wore into something she considered more 'in keeping' for the coming interview. Her choice was a prettily patterned sleeveless dress with lilacs on it. She'd bought it on the day her divorce had been finalised as a symbol of starting her life over again.

Unwinding her scrunched-up topknot, she brushed out her tousled hair to leave it lying loose against her bare shoulders. After that she applied the merest hint of make-up and sprayed a little of her favourite perfume behind her ears and on her wrists.

Her teeth worried at her lip as she checked her reflection in the mirror. It didn't really matter what she wore, she decided. It couldn't prevent her from looking like someone who'd pinched the last chocolate biscuit in the tin and felt guilty about it. As if to illustrate the fact, her cheeks were reddening even *before* Bastian arrived.

But there was no more time to take stock of things when the sudden pounding on the front door announced his arrival. Taking a deep breath in, she deliberately made her descent down the stairs a slow one. The last thing she wanted him to imagine was that she was in any way *eager* for this meeting.

But, opening the door, Lily felt her breath all but cease when she found herself confronted by nothing less than what was surely the most beautiful man on earth.

Wearing a white cambric shirt open at the neck and dark jeans, his hair naturally tousled, he gave her a slow, toe-curling smile. '*Buonasera*, Lily… I trust you've been expecting me?'

'Your prompt arrival is no surprise, if that's what you mean, *signor*?'

His gaze moved up and down her figure in the pretty lilac dress, not disguising the fact that he very much liked what he saw. 'Am I really so predictable, *mia dolcezza*?'

Dry-mouthed, she opened the door wider. 'You'd better come in.'

The simple Italian endearment had thrown her. Sucking in another steadying breath, she closed the door behind him and led the way into the living room. Before they sat down she saw his glance go to the bottle of red wine she'd left on the coffee table, alongside one of the cut-crystal wine glasses she'd found in a kitchen cabinet.

He frowned. 'The wine isn't for you, I take it?'

'Of course not—is it likely that I'd drink alcohol in my condition?'

'I'm glad you would not.'

Bastian meaningfully held her gaze for perhaps longer than was necessary. Deliberately drawing her glass of orange juice towards her, Lily couldn't help but gulp some down as she lowered herself into the armchair.

It didn't help cool her temperature one iota.

'The wine is for you.'

'How thoughtful of you—shall I pour?'

'Why don't you let me do it? After all, you're my guest.'

As he sat down opposite her on the tasteful sea-green couch, Lily couldn't help wincing when she remembered what had happened the last time he'd occupied similar seating in her living room…

Was the same thought going through *his* mind?

Quickly quashing the speculation, she deftly took out the cork that she'd removed earlier in readiness and carefully poured the ruby-red wine into his glass.

Leaning forward, he picked up the bottle to examine the label. Inclining his head in a gesture of approval, he commented, 'I see that you have very good taste in wine, Lily.'

Collecting her orange juice again, she clutched the glass even more tightly. 'I have to say that's high praise, coming from an Italian.'

After trying some of the wine, he remarked, 'But we are not alone in creating good wine. Many countries produce wine of exceptional quality these days. Anyway, moving on...we have something much more important to discuss, *si*?'

'I agree. Why don't you start us off?' she invited, her mouth immediately drying again in anticipation of what he might say.

She hadn't forgotten that he wanted to make their arrangement one of convenience, rather than because his feelings for her had grown.

'We need to discuss when our marriage will take place. My suggestion is that it should be quite soon.'

'So you're still set on marrying me, then?'

Immediately he positioned himself in front of her, and his unsettling glance challenged her.

'Do you really think I would have changed my mind over something this important? When you get to know me better you'll learn that I am a man of my word and that I *always* follow through on what I say.'

'Even if the other person involved isn't sure she agrees with you?'

'Seeing as you are still so unsure, Lily… I will just have to be sure for both of us.'

'How fortunate that you don't seem to doubt yourself.'

With an amused lift of his eyebrows he remarked, 'I have something else to say that will hopefully set your mind at rest. I have no intention of leaving you to manage the childcare on your own. I will hire us the best nanny I can find. And, as for parental occasions, I fully intend to be a supportive presence as often as I can. In fact I'll do my utmost to be there whenever you or my children need me. In conclusion, I will make a very good life for you all.'

His companion blinked in astonishment. 'You said children? It sounds like you've assumed we'll have more than one child together?'

His lips shaped into the most seductive and shameless grin known to woman.

'I do not assume anything. I merely speak from knowing how it is between us. Do you expect me to act as if I don't desire you?'

As he spoke Bastian removed her glass from between her fingers and drew her up onto her feet. It seemed as though in that moment the sound of her racing heartbeat drowned out any other sound. Already her blood was moving like molten lava as it throbbed sluggishly through her veins.

'Marriage isn't just about desire, though, is it?' she breathed huskily. 'It's about…it's about…'

Anything more she wanted to say was crushed into silence by his lips hungrily laying claim to hers. When his hot silken tongue swept inside the velvet landscape of her mouth she couldn't deny she'd been aching for his touch from the moment she'd seen him again.

Her response was automatic. She didn't hesitate to wrap her arms around him and feel the strength of his hard-honed muscles so close to the surface under his shirt. So intense were her feelings that they dangerously threatened to sweep away every last bit of common sense she possessed. She found herself forgetting everything but the joy of knowing he didn't easily want to let her go, and the memory of their urgent sensual coupling inevitably made her eager to experience more of the same.

But then, just as though she'd suddenly

been blinded by the sun, she dizzyingly came to her senses. In the next instant she found herself firmly pushing him away.

Her lover's deep brown eyes looked bemused. 'Are you intent on pretending that you don't want this?' he drawled.

'I'm not trying to pretend anything.' Abruptly, she folded her arms. 'It's just that we shouldn't give in to our carnal desires so easily. It's already had a serious consequence.'

'I don't just want your body, Lily. Didn't you hear me when I said I intend to marry you?'

She sighed. 'I heard. I also heard that you don't want a real marriage, but one of convenience. That doesn't make my decision any easier. It's a decision that will undoubtedly affect both our lives, and I need to know I'm doing the right thing. I've already told you that I made one huge mistake in marrying a man I didn't really know, and I don't want to make another. Especially not when I'm having a child.'

His expression fierce, Bastian compelled her to look at him. 'This is *my* child too, Lily—don't forget that.'

Startled by his possessive tone, she honestly didn't know what to do right then. Her senses were in turmoil. Yet she knew she didn't want a man who regarded her as some kind of possession and in so doing didn't consider her feelings. After what had happened with Marc she'd be a fool to forget that Bastian wasn't interested in having a more meaningful relationship. He'd already told her he wasn't expecting a romantic attachment...

Seeking distraction, she started to walk away towards the kitchen, thinking to calm herself by bringing in the snacks she'd prepared earlier.

However, her charismatic guest had other ideas.

Lightly catching her arm, he said, his tone more thoughtful than it had been previously, 'I realise that perhaps I should have made you a proper proposal. As yet, I know I haven't given you that. To make things right between us, I'm asking you now, Lily. Will you marry me?'

'I've already told you this isn't easy for me to decide.'

He blew out a frustrated breath. 'Look... I'll be frank with you. When I was younger

I was briefly engaged to a woman I thought myself in love with. Clearly not feeling the same, she betrayed me with a colleague. To add insult to injury, I found them in bed together—in my flat. I'd given her a key so she could let herself in. After that...' He shrugged and glanced away. 'After that I vowed I would never entertain the idea of having a serious relationship again.'

'That must have hurt. But what did you do after that? Ensure that your relationships were platonic?'

'Not quite—after all, I'm only human.' A corner of his mouth drew up into his cheek in amusement. 'But, returning to my proposal, I will ask you once again, Lily. Will you agree to marry me and be my wife?'

Hot colour surged into her face. 'I'm still uncertain, Bastian. This is just too serious to decide on quickly.'

'Marriage *is* a serious thing, I agree. But, like I said before, if we explicitly set out the terms of our contract we'll both know what we can and can't expect from one another and therefore we're unlikely to be disappointed.'

'You sound so certain that we'll be able to stick to the terms...'

'I am.'

Even as she listened to him Lily knew the time for deliberating further was gone. A person could think on a subject for far too long and just end up feeling hopelessly confused. And in the meantime her baby's wellbeing and future was at stake.

'I have to put my child's welfare before my own,' she said solemnly, 'so I guess my answer has to be yes, Bastian. I *will* agree to marry you and be your wife.'

Seeing satisfaction light his eyes, she experienced a genuine surge of pleasure at making the right decision for once.

But just after she'd given him her reply doubts once again started to besiege her...

A few nights after making their momentous decision to marry, and arranging their wedding date, Bastian agreed to give Lily some space in order to finish her current illustrative assignment before they wed. But his sense of being satisfied with his decision to marry was to be shaken by an unexpected event.

At home one evening, having just finished work in the olive groves, he had a panicked phone call from his father's housekeeper, Dolores.

'Signor Carrera—you must come to the house quickly! Your father has pain in his chest again and I'm afraid he might be having another heart attack!'

Swearing under his breath, Bastian slammed out through the door to his car parked outside. The vehicle flew down the dirt tracks and Tarmac roads to the house that anyone who saw Alberto regularly knew as home from home, because they were always guaranteed a welcome there.

He didn't think much beyond that. He definitely wouldn't go down the terrifying route of imagining that he was in danger of losing the man who meant the world to him...

When he arrived, Dolores immediately ushered him into the kitchen. Alberto was slumped in a rocking chair with a cushion behind his back and he was sweating profusely. As he strode towards the older man, whose greying hair was coiling damply to his brow, he demanded urgently over his shoulder as to whether the housekeeper had rung for an ambulance.

'*Si, signor.* It is on its way. I have been trying to give your father some water, but he doesn't seem able to swallow.'

Bastian hardly heard her. He was crouching down beside the older man and smoothing back his hair. Then, taking his father's hand in his, he assured him that everything was going to be all right, that they were blessed enough to be able to pay for the very best of care and he would soon be back on his feet and giving Dolores merry hell when her cooking didn't come up to scratch.

He heard the older woman sniff, as though she was finding it hard to hold back the tears.

Giving his son a painful half-smile, Alberto whispered, *'Lei e una cuoca terribile!' She is a terrible cook.* He tried to laugh but ended up nearly choking.

Bastian instantly brought him further forward in the chair, in a bid to help him clear his throat, and began to thump on his back. It was at that very moment they heard the distinctive sound of an ambulance siren.

Bastian was emotionally wrung out and numb with fatigue. The day's events had conspired to give him some of the most stressful few hours of his life. Now it was three in the morning, and he'd stayed at his father's bedside since the ambulance had brought him to the hospital.

Thankfully Alberto was now sleeping soundly, in a private room, and Bastian had been assured by the heart specialist who'd attended him that he was going to be all right. He would pull through. He needed plenty of rest and the professional care of his medical team.

But it was hard to believe that things would improve when his father looked so ill and was struggling to breathe. Now, having been put through all the various tests he'd needed, he had been fitted with an oxygen mask and it seemed to his son that he was rallying. But he wouldn't go home until he was convinced that he wouldn't take a turn for the worst as soon as his back was turned.

By the time he *did* head for home he knew he couldn't return to an empty house. It was only when he automatically found himself parking outside Lily's place that he realised her house had always been the only destination he'd had in mind...

'Bastian...it's nearly four in the morning. What's happened? Is something wrong?'

Beneath an open silky green robe that was decorated with slim-stemmed flowers, she was wearing a short cream nightgown that paid homage to her shapely slim legs, and she had clearly had got straight out of bed to answer the door. Her fair hair was prettily dishevelled and she was still rubbing the sleep from her incandescent green eyes.

He couldn't imagine that a more delectable sight existed.

'My father's in hospital with a suspected heart attack.'

Unable to help himself, he let his voice break then, and he sensed the tears he hadn't been able to hold back since he'd left Alberto's bedside temporarily blurring his vision.

Seeing that he was clearly in some distress, Lily opened the door wider, softly remarking, 'I'm so sorry to hear that. What do you need? If there's anything I can do to help you know I won't hesitate.'

'I don't want to be in the house alone. Can I stay here for the rest of the night with you? That's the only help I need.'

He heard a softly released inward gasp before she answered, 'Then let's go upstairs.'

CHAPTER SIX

HE'D MADE LOVE to her voraciously into the remaining hours of the morning. There had been no time for any demonstrations of finesse. Bastian had been hostage to the kind of urgent primal need that could present itself when someone was faced with the threat of death, and he had instinctively sought an affirmation of life to counteract it. The fear that had eaten him up at seeing his father so ill again had been tangible. Consequently he'd been a little less gentle than he could have been when his body had claimed Lily's.

Afterwards he'd apologised profusely, murmuring over and over again, *'Sono cosi dispiaciuto...'* I'm so sorry. Then he'd kissed her from her head to her toes, as if to soothe any hurts he might have unwittingly inflicted and to let her know that he genuinely cared about how she felt.

Lily had been utterly swept away by him. Even in her most private dreams she'd never ever been able to conjure up a lover with the devastating touch of Bastian. But as she'd driven her fingers into his richly dark hair it had come to her that he was like a flint that could turn the merest spark of her desire into a conflagration, no matter what the situation or where they were.

It was as though their need for each other was unquenchable and there was nothing that could slake their thirst. Their shared desire was constantly simmering, ready to catch fire the moment they caught sight of each other.

Naked, and tangled in the single cotton sheet that was left on the bed after their passionate lovemaking, Lily turned carefully onto her side and met Bastian's sexily drowsy gaze. As she looked at him she whispered, 'We really ought to try and get some sleep. You've already been up most of the night at the hospital.'

'I know,' he murmured. 'Forgive me for keeping you awake so long, *tesoro.*'

She didn't miss the glint of regret in his deep brown eyes. Laying his hand against her belly, that he must surely see was becoming gently rounded, he asked, 'You are feeling all right? I mean…the baby is doing well?'

'We're both doing just fine. Don't give yourself anything else to worry about. You have enough to think about with your dad being ill.'

'*Si*…but you and the *bambino* will soon be my family too, remember?'

Her insides turned over at the statement. Her mind immediately returned to his intention of legalising their union, and she knew the idea still made her nervous. In light of her previous failed marriage to Marc it was understandable that she was guarded about making another emotionally costly mistake.

'And, speaking of the baby, in order to ensure you get the very best of care I'd like you to see a private obstetrician. Do you agree?'

'Of course, but…'

'You seem hesitant?'

'It's just that I've already seen a local doctor and I was quite satisfied with him.'

'That may be so, Lily, but that's not good enough for me.'

'Do you really want to go to the expense of paying for private care when it's not necessary?'

'Frugality has dulled your senses, sweetheart. I don't need to think about the cost. All I want is the best care for my fiancée and my baby. To that end, I will gladly pay a fortune.'

'But—'

'No more buts. I will make the necessary calls tomorrow.'

He drew her protectively against his warm, muscular chest and planted a kiss on the top of her head. Right then she had never felt more as if her wellbeing mattered. Given her history, that had to be a first.

Knowing that she'd given him the satisfaction he craved when he'd most needed it, she hoped it had helped him to set his fears and worries aside for a while. Sensing that he'd fallen into a gentle doze, she started to relax. As she closed her eyes and started to drift off to sleep herself, she was reassured that at least she and Bastian shared a strong physical attraction and he was more than willing to meet his parental responsibilities when he became a father.

Yet somehow, before she fell asleep, thoughts of her marriage to Marc drifted into her mind. Yes, she'd initially had high hopes of a secure future with the handsome broker, but if she'd loved him at all it had been as a friend, and not because theirs was a love match in any sense of the word.

During their first few meetings they'd shared a few chaste kisses, and Lily had been charmed by his politeness and thoughtfulness. But, if she was honest, she *had* been concerned about his lack of passion. She'd pondered that maybe it was because she didn't know how to turn a man on and her lack of experience was too evident. And she'd mused on the fact that surely it was natural that a soon-to-be married couple should have more physical contact then they had.

The situation hadn't improved—even though Marc had promised that their wedding night would be everything she'd dreamed it would be, and that he was holding back on physical contact till then so she would enjoy their special night even more.

But the fact was he'd knowingly deceived her. Their wedding night had turned out to be an unmitigated disaster. He couldn't consummate their marriage, he'd confessed, because in truth he wasn't attracted to her in 'that way'.

It had seemed as if her worst fears had

come true. Feeling like an out-and-out fail-
ure, she'd demanded to know why he hadn't
told her this before? Why he had led her to
believe they could be happy together?

Breaking down, he had finally told her that
he loved and respected her, but he was gay.

Glad that that bittersweet episode in her life
was now firmly behind her, Lily reflected on
the instantaneous hunger that she and Bastian
had shared. Was it any wonder that her pent-
up feelings and lack of physical attention had
exploded into a demanding need she could no
longer ignore, causing her to spontaneously
have sex with him?

Nothing that anyone had told her, or that
she'd read in any erotic work of fiction, could
have prepared her for the reality of such a
thrilling event. And, little did her lover realise, the event had far more significance than
just the fact he'd made her pregnant...

Bastian's heart thudded when he opened his
eyes. Full daylight was streaming into the
room and he realised that he wasn't in his
own bed but in Lily's. A jolt of disappointment churned in his gut when he saw that
she'd already risen and gone downstairs. Her

scent was all over him, and more to the point he *wanted* her again. Why had she so quickly deserted him?

Glancing irritably down at his watch, he saw the time and at exactly the same moment remembered that his father was in hospital.

'Damn!'

He could hardly believe he'd slept so long. He urgently needed to know how things were.

Reaching for his mobile from atop the bedside cabinet, he saw it was thankfully devoid of any new messages. Sighing with relief, he composed a quick text to the doctor, asking for an update, and then sent a longer one to his dad, telling him not to worry, that he was in good hands and that Bastian would come in and see him later that morning. He finished by asking if there was anything he wanted brought in for him.

After that he headed for the shower, and saw that Lily had left him a stack of pristinely fresh towels on the artisan chair positioned outside the door.

It didn't take him long to freshen up, and as soon as he was done and dressed he went downstairs. Heavy-eyed, and still fastening his leather belt round his jeans, he scented the welcome aroma of coffee brewing. Finding his lover in the kitchen, dressed in a simple yellow cotton dress with her feet tantalisingly bare, he saw that she was busy frying some bacon at the stove.

The woman seemed to know instinctively just how to please him.

Stealing up behind her, Bastian caught her by the hips and turned her around to face him. '*Buongiorno...*'

Planting a warm kiss at the side of her neck, he saw the tell-tale bite mark he'd left behind last night and felt his blood start to heat at the memory.

Breathing in her beguiling scent, he smiled slowly into her eyes. 'You were in a hurry to get up before me. I'd very much hoped we could get reacquainted before we had coffee this morning.'

She looked endearingly self-conscious, and a touch of crimson swept into her cheeks. It made him realise that one of the most appealing things about her was her modesty.

'I got up early because I wanted to make us some breakfast. I hope you like eggs and bacon?'

'I like whatever you care to give me, sweetheart, especially if it's made by your own fair hands.'

She turned back to the stove, but not before saying, 'I can see you've inherited some of Alberto's charm.'

When he didn't immediately reply, Lily set the sizzling bacon aside and wiped her hands on a nearby tea towel.

Her brow crumpled concernedly. 'Have you heard anything…from the hospital, I mean?'

'No, I haven't. I sent a couple of texts but I haven't had any replies yet. I think I'll just go outside and ring—see if I can speak to the doctor personally. Can you put breakfast on hold for a couple of minutes?'

'Of course. I'll pop it in the oven. Take as much time as you need.'

When he returned it was with a great sense of relief. Dropping down onto a nearby chair, so that he could easily observe Lily as she worked in the kitchen, Bastian confided, 'He's not out of the woods yet, but his doctor told me he's doing much better than expected. He's sleeping right now, but I was told I can go in and see him this afternoon. Would you like to come with me? I'm sure it would please him.'

Lily flushed, as he had suspected she would. 'Of course I'd like to see him, but...'

'I see that yet again you're searching for an excuse.'

'It's not an excuse. It's just that it's only natural he'll want to see you on your own first. Perhaps I can come in some other time soon?'

'What's on your mind? Tell me.' Straight away he went over to her and took her in his arms.

With a heartfelt sigh she replied, 'I'm not family. I'm not even a close friend.'

'I disagree.' A lock of hair was drifting very close to her eyes and he gently swept it aside. 'You are having my baby and we are soon going to be married. I can't think of anything that epitomises "family" more than that.'

As if uneasy with this statement, she carefully stepped out of his hold and briskly wiped her hands on the apron she was wearing.

'I'm sure you're right. Now, why don't you go and sit down and I'll bring you your breakfast? After that we can decide when we're going to leave for the hospital.'

* * *

She had changed out of her cheerful sun dress and replaced it with a much more demure blue tunic over white linen trousers. The only decoration she wore was the dainty gold cross and chain that had been an eighteenth birthday present from her mother.

Lily didn't wear the jewellery very often, because it reminded her that her parent had long since moved away to Scotland, announcing that she wanted to live a new life and put the old one behind her.

Lily's father had finally walked out on Lily's mother after years of persistent arguments over his infidelities, leaving her to raise their daughter alone, and she had very few happy memories of their life together. The irony was that her mother was living in her new place with another man and was helping to raise *his* child from a previous relationship.

Had it never crossed her mind that her own child was bereft of her love and care? Lily doubted it.

It wasn't surprising that people were cynical about the possibility of having a relationship that stayed the course. To her mind, both her parents had deserted her long before she'd experienced any kind of stability. Was it surprising that her nature had developed into such an insecure one?

However, she put all thoughts of her past aside as she and Bastian took the elevator to the topmost floor of the hospital, where the private suites were situated. After walking down an elegant corridor that was decorated with artistic prints, to her surprise he caught her hand as he opened a door labelled 'The Da Vinci Room'.

He hadn't said very much during their car journey, but she sensed that despite his putting on a brave face worry and fear about his dad were never far away. However, his trademark dazzling smile had started to form even before his gaze met his father's.

Still looking a little frail after his unexpected health scare, and attended by a tall, slim uniformed nurse who had clearly just taken his temperature, Alberto almost did a double-take when he saw Lily enter the room with his son. However, his attention was soon diverted as Bastian approached the bedside.

'Hey, it's good to see you looking so much better. I see you no longer have to wear the oxygen mask? That has to be a good sign.'

The younger man enveloped him in a careful but loving hug, so as not to dislodge the wires and tubes he was attached to, and added mischievously, 'I'm told you're driving the medical staff crazy with all your demands! No doubt they assumed a man of your age would be much more manageable and not give them any trouble.'

His father's eyes crinkled in amusement. 'I do not give anyone any trouble. I am like a teddy bear.'

Bastian laughed.

Surveying her patient, the nurse briskly interjected. 'I will leave you alone now, and give you some privacy with your son, Signor Carrera—but not for long. Your doctor is coming to take some more tests in half an hour.'

After attaching her latest recorded assessment to a clipboard at the end of the bed she left the room, shutting the door noiselessly behind her.

Alberto immediately swung his gaze to Lily, who had positioned herself further away from the bed, mindful of not being intrusive.

The older Italian gave no sign of noticing her slight unease and warmly invited her,

'Come and sit closer to me, *tesoro*... I did not expect your visit, but it gives me much pleasure to see you.'

'Bastian said I should come. I hope you don't mind? I was worried about you...'

Taking her hand in his, he smiled. 'I am doing much better than they expected, my doctor tells me. Now all I want is to be back at home with the people I love and care about.'

'I know your son feels the same, *signor*... I mean, he wants you to get well and come home soon.'

Stealing a shy glance up at her landlord, who was now sitting on the edge of his father's bed, the strong muscles in his thighs highlighted by his black jeans, she was reassured to have him smile back at her.

Then, focusing on the other man, he said, 'As well as wanting you home, I have some good news to share with you.'

'Oh? What is that, son?'

Before the younger Carrera replied Lily's heartbeat was already racing as she realised what he was going to say. They hadn't even *discussed* telling his father about the situation yet. To reveal it now, at his hospital bedside, didn't just mean she was committed to going through with it—it meant there could be no going back…

'Lily and I are going to be married.'

For a long moment all the colour seemed to drain from Alberto's face. Then, quickly recovering, he started to beam. 'You're serious? When did all this happen?'

'Pretty soon after we met.'

'But this is the most wonderful thing I have ever heard! Already I can feel my weakened heart mending.'

Drawing Lily's hand to his lips, he kissed it as though it were some priceless treasure, then put it down beside him on the bed as if to keep her close.

'We felt an attraction at our very first meeting,' Bastian explained. 'And our feelings grew stronger each time we met.'

His tone sounded surprisingly assured. It didn't seem to contain so much as a shred of doubt.

'Quite soon it blossomed into something deeper. Now we want to make a life together.'

Feeling unexpected warmth flood into her chest, Lily found herself wishing his words could be true. That they *were* going to be wed because they'd fallen in love and couldn't for a single moment envisage living their lives without each other.

'I can hardly believe my dearest wish is going to come true at last,' Alberto remarked, lightly squeezing her hand. 'I confess I began to think you would be a single man for the rest of your life, Bastian. I know it must have been hard for you getting close to women growing up without your mother. If she'd lived she would have been a wonderful example to you of how loving a woman can be. But Dolores always said you would meet the right woman when you were ready...that God would take care of things...and now Lily has come into your life. I should never have doubted it.'

'All that is well and good, but you mustn't over-excite yourself. The last thing I want is for your blood pressure to go sky-high and for you to have to stay in hospital even longer.'

'It won't be like that, son. Not now that I have something unexpectedly wonderful to live for—I *guarantee* it. But...tell me...what made you decide on marriage so suddenly?'

Lily almost held her breath as she waited to hear Bastian's answer.

'We are going to have a baby,' he said quietly, spearing his hand through his hair and giving her a lop-sided smile. 'Lily is pregnant.'

It was tough saying goodbye to his father, knowing he'd only just embarked on what was probably a long road to recovery after suffering a second heart attack. Bastian could will him better as much as he liked, but he knew that no one was ever guaranteed the outcome they desired.

Still, the older man had been noticeably cheered by news of the coming baby and the couple's intended marriage. He'd always had a soft spot for Lily. So now his son had to put his mind to organising a wedding that was in keeping with the family's status and also ensure that his bride-to-be wasn't so overwhelmed by the idea that she ran away rather than face it and enjoy it.

As much as he wanted to get to know Lily properly, she was still somewhat of a mystery to him. But the practicalities of their union were looming large, and suddenly overshadowing everything else. However, Bastian couldn't deny that he'd started to develop some unexpectedly powerful feelings towards her. They had slammed into him like a bullet train and he was afraid to explore what they might mean.

Putting his fears aside, the next morning he took Lily to his house in the hills. The day was warm with an accompanying mild breeze as the car climbed the steep roadway to take them to the panoramic vista that he loved. He'd named the house he'd had built there Buona Stella—Lucky Star—when after several years of consistently dedicated work he'd started to make his mark on the Carrera family fortunes. He loved coming here almost as much as he loved going home to his dad's place.

The air was drenched with the scent of aromatic herbs and spices and a medley of plants and flowers native to the country he was so proud of. There was even a winding path that led to an olive grove. But most of all the house itself was breathtakingly lovely, and imposed itself graciously on the landscape as though it had always been there.

He'd spared no expense in making it even more beautiful. Constructed in traditional stone and marble, it had been brought it up to date with plenty of modern features, such as state-of-the-art bathrooms, two spacious living rooms with access to the latest technology, and a cinema room so that he and his guests could watch and discuss films together. He'd even installed an impressive library, because books had always been one of his passions too.

But his fiancée was unusually quiet as she dutifully followed him from room to room, and that disturbed him. He wished he knew what was on her mind.

'Let's take a pause for a few minutes.'

Guiding her to stop just outside the entrance to the kitchen, he let his gaze finally settle on the lovely features that he never grew tired of, his lips curving into an encouraging smile.

'Talk to me. I'd like to know what you're thinking.'

'You mean about the house?'

He raised a quizzical eyebrow. 'Yes. Would you be happy living here when we marry?'

Hectic colour instantly flooded her cheeks. 'I'm sure *any* woman would love to live in a place like this.'

'So why am I doubtful and thinking you're not exactly pleased about the prospect?'

'I don't know why you think that.' Her upper lip trembled a little, and she folded her arms over her cream cotton sweater as if wanting to protect herself against some potential slight or hurt.

'Perhaps I'm concerned that you still don't trust what I say, Lily?'

'Trust develops over time, doesn't it? We're just—we're just starting to get to know one another.'

'That's true… Leaving that alone for a moment, since we should be discussing the wedding, I need to know if you'll be inviting your parents to the ceremony. You haven't mentioned them at all.'

Her green eyes widened in surprise. 'Does it matter to you if they come or don't come?'

'As a matter of fact it does. Besides, what parent wouldn't want to be at their daughter's wedding?'

'It's pure fantasy, if you believe that. Not all parents are as loving and caring as your dad, Bastian. My dad walked out on my mum when I was nine. I didn't know it until later, but he'd been regularly cheating on her with other women. That's why they were always arguing. One day he just got up and left. Presumably he'd had enough of the rows. After that…'

Shrugging a slim shoulder, she glanced away, as if she couldn't bear to entertain the hurtful memories it evoked.

'After that, my mum just got on with her life as best she could. She took care of me, but she never expressed much joy or pleasure in anything. No doubt my dad's infidelities must have scarred her. Then, when I was eighteen, she met a man who was temporarily working in London. He was an engineer and he came from Edinburgh. When his contract came to an end he went back to Scotland and my mum went with him. So as for my relationship with my parents…we hardly stay in touch. A couple of years ago, when I told them I was marrying a stockbroker, all my mum said at the time was, "Good—at least I know he'll be able to take care of you." The truth is I'm sure she was glad I'd finally be out of her hair. Does that answer your question as to whether they'll be coming to our wedding or not?'

Feeling as if he'd stumbled into a hornets' nest, Bastian stared at Lily, feeling stunned. 'I'm not like your father was, Lily. I'm not someone who cheats on the woman in his life and I never would.'

'I can only hope that that's true. I wouldn't like to go through what my mum did.'

Frustrated that he couldn't immediately convince her, he remarked, 'You say your father left when you were nine? Isn't that when you went on that school trip and woke your teacher in the night to tell her you couldn't sleep?'

'So?'

'I think your dad's leaving affected you much more than you care to admit, Lily. Am I right?'

She nodded mutely and a lone tear slid down her cheek. It was quickly followed by a steady stream.

Bastian could hardly bear to see her cry. In less than a heartbeat he had her in his arms. Pushing his strong supple fingers into her hair, he brought her head down to his chest.

Touching his lips to the silken strands on her scalp as though she were a distressed child, he murmured gently, 'It will all be okay, *tesorino*. It's perfectly natural to cry and express your grief. It's better to let your feelings out than to bottle them up inside.

It sounds as though your parents were too caught up in their own troubles to give you the support you needed. But that can change, you know?'

Sniffing, she pushed back her hair and glanced up at him. 'Can it?' she asked croakily. 'They don't even really know me. I'm not sure if they even *want* to.'

Laying a hand against her dampened cheek, he said, 'I doubt if that's true. I cannot imagine a mother or father who wouldn't love a daughter as beautiful and talented as you are, Lily. You should talk to them again. You need to tell them about the baby as well as the wedding.'

'You really think so?'

There was still a suggestion of doubt and uncertainty in her voice.

'You don't need me to tell you what to do,' he breathed. 'You just need to start having some faith in making your own decisions.'

'You're right.' Flushing a little, as though suddenly backed into a corner, she motioned towards the open doorway. 'Would you like to show me the rest of the house?'

'Of course.'

Gesturing for her to go ahead of him, Bastian followed her, wishing he could knock down that wall she'd erected around herself and get her to see what he suspected was a very competent and able woman underneath. See that there was no need for her to believe she was any less important than anyone else.

When they went through to the kitchen at last, she took him aback when she exclaimed, 'Oh, Bastian, this is wonderful. Who wouldn't love to cook in a space like this? I'm sure your mother would have adored it if she'd lived.'

The comment stunned him with how apt it was. His father had often told him how much his wife had loved cooking, and Lily's thoughtful remark emphatically cheered him.

Without hesitation he drew her against him, delighting at the way her feminine curves felt against his body as he captured her lips in a warm, heartfelt kiss.

Startled, she didn't hide the pleasure in her lustrous green eyes. 'What was that for?'

'I thought about my mother a lot when I had this area designed. I didn't know her, but sometimes I feel like I can sense her presence… I like to think that she was giving me some guidance.'

'Well…'

She moved her fingertips down over his shirt, and although her touch was infinitely gentle he could still feel her heat radiating through the material.

'One thing's for sure…she would have been very proud at the way her son has turned out.'

Expelling a sigh and smoothing his palm over her hair, he remarked huskily, 'If you keep on saying such nice things to me we won't get round to discussing the wedding at all.'

'Oh? Why's that?'

'Because if matters follow their usual course we'll give in to something even *more* pleasurable and everything else will be forgotten.'

CHAPTER SEVEN

As it transpired, they *did* discuss the wedding. But every time she met Bastian's seductive brown eyes and saw the desire that was never far away when they were together Lily found it hard to curtail her feelings of lust and longing.

If she'd imagined that pregnancy would call a halt to sexual desire then she couldn't have been more wrong.

And now, as if the prospect of their marital union didn't already feel like a mountain to climb, Bastian had informed her that he'd arranged for them to visit the family's private jeweller the next day, to look at a selection of wedding ring designs.

The Carreras had a *private jeweller*? Yet again she was reminded of how wealthy and important the family she was marrying into was and her stomach flipped. What would

Bastian's relations and friends think when they met her and found out that she was no one significant?

By the time they got back to her house her energy was exhausted by the see-saw of emotions. First of all at the idea of getting married in the ancient historical church that Bastian's family had frequented for centuries. being a fitting enough bride for the heir to the Carrera fortune, and walking up the aisle with everyone probably suspecting or knowing that she was pregnant.

They were none of them small concerns.

She only hoped she would be able to set them aside for a while and garner enough motivation to finish some of her book illustrations.

As she opened the front door her handsome husband-to-be startled her by catching her arm and turning her round to face him.

'I can sense that you're still not at ease.' He frowned. 'I realise that everything that's been happening must seem quite formidable to you, but I'd like you to remember that I'm doing all this for you and the baby.'

'And what about *you*, Bastian…? Are you honestly happy to be marrying a woman you barely know because you made her pregnant and now find you have to support her?'

'Don't you listen to *anything* I say?' For an unsettling moment, a flash of electrifying anger flared in his eyes. 'I told you I'm not a man who runs away from his responsibilities. I am marrying you and supporting this child because I *want* to. No one is forcing me.'

Lily shivered. If only he'd said he wanted to marry her because he loved her, instead of still leaving her with the impression that he was merely doing his duty.

But even as she entertained the thought she knew she shouldn't delude herself if she didn't want to invite any more hurt and disappointment.

'I heard what you said and I'm grateful. Really, I am.'

Clearly dubious, he released her to sweep his hand restlessly through his hair. 'I don't expect you to be grateful. I just wish…'

'What do you wish?'

'Never mind.' His tone was dismissive. 'It's not important. Look, I need to get back to work. I have a pressing meeting with some of my workers this afternoon.'

'That's fine with me. There's no need for you to stay any longer. We've discussed the most important things, haven't we?'

'Yes. I suppose we have.'

'And I want to say if you need me to go to the hospital with you to see your dad later, just give me a call.'

'I wouldn't dream of it. You look dead on your feet. There's been a lot for you to take in today, and you're probably anxious to have some time to deal with your own work… hmm?'

Reaching out a hand, he lightly stroked his fingers down her cheek, and once again Lily's heart leapt at his touch. What she wouldn't give to have some more time with him alone…

But in the next instant he'd moved away, his smile regretful. 'I'll see you tomorrow, around midday—I'll pick you up for our meeting with the jeweller. Make sure you get some rest tonight and don't overdo things. *Arrivederci*.'

Sighing, she watched him walk past the bed of new blooms she'd planted in the hope that they'd symbolise a new beginning for her and the baby. But he wasn't to know that was her reason for planting them. Why hadn't she told him?

He didn't even glance at them. Instead he got into his car and drove away...

She had dark circles beneath her eyes from another sleepless night. She had tried to drink a cup of coffee to help perk herself up, but had ended up tipping it down the sink because in her pregnant state even the smell of it made her feel queasy.

But, remembering the reason for her lack of sleep, Lily knew she would have to deal with things as soon as possible before she backed out. So it was with trepidation that she rang Bastian on his mobile.

He wouldn't like what she had to say, but *he* was the one who'd told her she needed to have more faith in her decisions and to believe in herself. Now she was going to put his advice into practice.

'Lily... To what do I owe the honour?' he greeted her, sounding pleased that she'd phoned.

Taking a deep breath in and out again, and staring out through the window at her sunlit patio, she answered, 'I need to talk to you about something.'

'Are you and the baby okay?'

'Yes, we're fine.'

'Good. So, what do you want to tell me?'

'It's just that I—I want to talk to you about the wedding…'

'Didn't we discuss that yesterday?'

'We did…but—'

Her tone couldn't help but ring alarm bells for Bastian and he tensed. 'What *about* the wedding?'

'I've changed my mind about something.'

The excoriating point of what felt like something akin to a deadly arrow hit him squarely in the gut.

Hardly knowing how he formed the words, he snapped, 'What do you mean, you've changed your mind about something? Are you saying you don't want to get married to me after all?'

She was taking too long to answer, and fear and impatience stole a march on any chance of his staying calm.

'For goodness' sake…what are you playing at, Lily?'

Hearing her softly released breath, he felt

as though she were standing next to him. If he shut his eyes he knew he'd be able to conjure up the incredibly seductive scent of her body... But all the things that made him feel good about her only made things *worse* for him right then.

'I still want to marry you, Bastian—of course I do,' she explained. 'Just not in the traditional way. I mean, not in the church your family have attended for millennia, with me wearing a posh gown that probably cost too much money and wearing a ring that I'd be terrified of losing every time I wore it because you'd spent a small fortune on it.'

The words tumbled from her lips as though she feared she would run out of air. But, pausing at last, she sucked in another breath and then continued.

'I'm not the kind of woman who likes a fuss. I'd be far happier if we could just get married in a beautiful garden or out in nature. We could have a celebrant marry us and after the ceremony maybe have a nice meal at a local restaurant. That's what I'd like for our wedding—at least, that's what I'd *prefer.*'

Bastian had wandered into the dining room, where he more often than not went with a cup of coffee when he had things on his mind. Pulling out a chair from the table, he sat down, his fingers gripping the phone tightly against his ear. Staring down at the grain in the burnished wood, he couldn't hide his disbelief at what he'd just heard.

'What is the *matter* with you?' he burst out. 'I'm offering you the kind of wedding that most women can only dream of and you're more or less telling me that it's not good enough? That instead of properly celebrating our union, in a church that has been the cornerstone of my family's faith for centuries, where our friends and family will join us to witness the occasion, you want us to play it small—as if the event is of no importance at all!'

The silence that followed was painful.

'I'm shocked that you think *how* we get married isn't important to me—because it is. It's just that the church and everything else might be significant for you and your family, Bastian, but it didn't play a big part in the way *I* was raised. I already told you what it was like for me. But, putting that aside, it doesn't mean that I don't appreciate beauty and reverence. God knows I'm thankful for *any* good fortune I'm blessed with. For instance, I'm especially grateful that as the father of my baby you want to marry me. I just don't want to be a hypocrite, having to pretend I go along with a big fancy wedding.'

His heart was thumping hard. The last time he'd been so emotionally churned up about a woman was when he'd walked in on his cheating ex, Marissa, in bed with a business rival. The image had sickened him and it had taken a long time for him to forget it.

Lily wasn't cheating on him. She was merely expressing her preference about where and how their wedding should be conducted. But the strength of his emotions right then wouldn't allow him to be remotely reasonable. Telling him that she didn't want what he was offering was tantamount to belittling him in the worst possible way.

'So you think it hypocritical to accept what I intended to be my gift to you…a beautiful wedding, the memory of which I hoped you'd cherish always?'

'What? Is that what you—? *Oh, Bastian.*'

On a sob, Lily ended the call…

* * *

No matter how many times he rang her, she didn't pick up. Finally, nearly driven crazy by the thought of what she might do when he remembered she had a tendency to blame herself when things went wrong, he got into his luxury four-by-four and drove straight over to her place.

There was no sign of the small tangerine-coloured car she drove.

Already knowing it was a pointless exercise, he rang the doorbell. As he'd expected, it chimed uselessly.

Blinking up into the flawlessly blue sky, he swore vehemently beneath his breath. Where the blazes had she gone? She'd broken off their conversation without explanation and he knew he'd upset her. Now she was probably driving around barely knowing where she was going because she was too distraught to think clearly.

Finally, deciding on a more pragmatic approach, he rang his jeweller Gianni and told him their meeting would have to be postponed. After that he drove into the local town to see if he could locate Lily in any of the shops and cafés. He would give her description to some of the locals and ask if anyone had seen her.

A woman who looked like *she* did surely wasn't so easy to forget catching sight of?

Having nearly worn herself out, walking up and down the sometimes steep inclines of the town's picturesque streets and getting a stitch in her side, Lily found a café and went inside. She was pleased to see that they had a selection of fruit teas as well as coffee, so she ordered some camomile and sat down in a window seat to stare out at the influx of tourists that mingled with the locals.

She took unexpected comfort in hearing snatches of their conversations, and occasionally their laughter as they went by. Sometimes she was glad to be a stranger in a town that wasn't her own. At least she could be anonymous.

But thoughts of Bastian never left her. Recalling the last thing he'd said to her—that he'd meant their wedding in the family church to be his gift to her and had hoped she would cherish the memory always—she knew it had utterly shaken her. It had been a bolt out of the blue, and the declaration she'd made beforehand—that she wanted a simple wedding and preferred not to have any fuss—now made her feel more than a little ashamed.

Bastian had already done so much for her and she'd acted as if she was throwing his kindness back in his face. How could she put things right again between them? She hadn't taken his calls because whatever she told him would be woefully inadequate. She needed more time to decide what to do.

It was then that it occurred to her to ring her mum. It had been a long time since they'd spoken, but perhaps now was exactly the right time to talk? Lily needed to hear the familiar voice of someone who had once upon a time known her better than anyone else, and God knew Jane Alexander had had plenty of experience in dealing with the vagaries of relationships.

By the time the call came to an end Lily was gratified that she had indeed done the right thing. Her mother had professed to being over the moon at hearing from her, and had asked why on earth she hadn't let her know she'd changed her mobile number?

The last time they'd spoken was when she'd been about to marry the stockbroker, Jane had reminded her, and she'd often worried about how things were going.

When Lily had told her they'd divorced, she'd gone silent for a moment. Then Lily had explained *why* it hadn't worked out and that Marc was gay.

'Why the hell didn't he tell you that in the first place?' Why string you along and pretend that he loved you?' her mother had asked.

'He *did* love me—but only as a friend. In truth, I often suspected he didn't want me physically, but I wasn't brave enough to challenge him about it. Yes, he *should* have told me the truth before we married, but he said he was afraid of losing my support and friendship if he did—that arrangements had gone too far. We should *never* have married—that much is clear to me now. Anyway, after a few months of living with me he fell in love with someone much more suitable. A man he'd met at a financial seminar. We agreed to part.'

'So where does all this leave *you*, Lily? I hope he compensated you financially for this?'

'He offered me alimony but I didn't accept. I accepted a one-off payment, though—and that, combined with the savings I already had, was enough to enable me to start my new life in Italy. And fortunately I've continued to have plenty of work.'

'Italy?'

'Don't worry, Mum, I'm really happy here. I'm living in a beautiful region called Abruzzo and the place I live in is near the beach. I've settled in well.'

'It seems you're full of surprises. How could I not know you're so adventurous? Don't worry about answering that. I shouldn't have left it so long to get to know you again, love.'

Lily could have said many things about how she felt about that, but she'd been intent on repairing some of the hurts from her past—not making matters worse.

'That's not all I have to tell you, Mum...'

It was then that she had told her mother that since moving to Italy she'd met someone else and was about to marry him. She was also pregnant. But Bastian was an entirely different proposition from Marc, she'd explained, and he wanted to do the right thing by her and the baby.

She'd finished the call with the revelation

that they were getting married in the exquisite ancient church that his family had attended for generations and he wanted her to invite her parents.

'I can only speak for myself right now, but I'd love to be there for you, sweetheart,' Jane had immediately replied. 'I know we have a lot of ground to make up, but I want to make amends. I just hope that this man of yours knows how lucky he is to have found you. You're a lovely girl, Lily, and you deserve only the best after all you've been through.'

'Thanks for that, Mum. The situation with Marc *did* hurt me. It knocked the stuffing out of me, to be honest. And somehow I believed that I was the one to blame for it all. I haven't always thought the best of myself...'

'Well, you should. You're not responsible for how other people behave—and that includes me and your dad. Don't you still do those wonderful illustrations and earn your living from them? Anyway, your dad and I *are* talking again, and we're both trying hard to come to terms with the past and put it behind us. I'm sure he'll want to come to the wedding too, if he knows you want him there.'

After such an encouraging revelation Lily hadn't hesitated in giving her mum all the details she wanted, including her new mobile number.

Her mother's final words before they'd ended the call were, 'I love you very much, darling, and I always have. I know I didn't give you the childhood you deserved, but I was so jealous and hurt because of your father's antics that I was consumed with my own troubles and lost sight of what was the most important thing of all…my *child.* I hope you'll give me the chance to make up for that a little with your own children?'

'I will. I love you too, Mum.'

Feeling as though a great weight had been lifted from her, Lily ordered another camomile tea and then checked her phone for any more missed calls from Bastian. As she tried to find his number the very effusive welcome to a customer from one of the young female baristas made her look up to see who the girl was greeting.

Wearing jeans and a plain white shirt, and making his usual arresting impression with his handsome face and tousled dark locks, Bastian was standing in front of the counter. After sharing some brief repartee with the girl, who looked as though she longed to have him stay and talk to her some more, he quickly moved his glance to scan the now crowded room.

His searching gaze didn't take long to find Lily. As their glances met and held she felt her heart gallop dizzyingly with excitement, but she couldn't seem to summon the welcoming smile she wanted. Knowing that she'd disappointed him, it wasn't easy.

The other customers seemed to have no such reticence. Smiles and greetings abounded as he neared. People drew back their chairs to let him get by as though he was some kind of celebrity, and she mused that the scene was a bit like the biblical parting of the waves. That was the mesmerising effect the man had on people.

Unconsciously her hand moved to rest on her belly. And she was having his baby.

His opening line wasn't the one she'd hoped for. Standing before her, his body temporarily shielding her from prying eyes, he demanded, low-voiced, 'Why in *hell* didn't you answer my calls?'

Inside, she wondered if he'd ever forgive her for the transgression.

'Don't ever do that to me again. I don't know what I would have done if I hadn't found you.'

His words were laced with underlying passion, and Lily intuited that he was more upset than angry. Deeply regretting that she'd worried him so much, she leant towards him and caught his hand.

'I never meant you to think I'd run away. I just—I just didn't know what to say to you.'

His jaw tightening as though he was barely able to contain his emotion, he replied, 'Let's get out of here. We'll go back to my place. At least I'll know you're safe there.'

'I was never in any danger. I just needed to think things over…to walk and get some air.'

'But now you look flushed and tired…as if you've needlessly exerted yourself. That's hardly going to help you *or* the baby, is it?'

Because she was wary of saying the wrong thing just then, Lily stayed silent. She let the charismatic Italian guide her up onto her feet, deciding to tell him later that she'd decided to go along with the church wedding after all and that she'd invited her parents.

She just hoped he still wanted that and didn't still believe she was being ungrateful in saying she wanted something different. She just hoped he hadn't changed his mind…

CHAPTER EIGHT

BASTIAN WAS ONLY too aware that he was treating Lily like spun glass…as though with one false move she might splinter and break. And, although he meant well, he realised that his too-protective attitude towards her was creating something of a chasm between them.

There had been no more falling into each other's arms at the drop of a hat and no more heated lovemaking. When he had found her that day in the café her appearance had alarmed him. She'd looked more fragile than he'd ever seen her look before and had been both nervous and wary of him when he'd appeared.

He *hated* it that she might feel that way around him. Had she ever felt that way about her ex? He wished he'd quizzed her more about her previous marriage. Had Marc cheated on her? Was that why her marriage had failed? More to the point, was she nervous because she feared he would treat her like her ex had?

Bastian felt a chill run down his spine. The memory of what Marissa had done to him had instigated a need in him never to give his heart to anyone again. Now Lily was sorely testing that vow.

Feeling concerned that recent events had taxed her too much, the first thing he'd done on reaching home was to organise a visit to a private obstetrician for a full examination. They hadn't had long to wait for an appointment, and just a couple of days later, on their visit to the exclusive maternity clinic, they'd been reassured by the news that all was progressing as it should.

But Lily had been advised that she needed to lessen her stress as much as possible and be mindful about making time for some proper rest during the day. She also needed to put on a little weight.

Bastian hadn't been able to help glancing at her in concern when he'd heard that, but his bewitching fiancée had merely smiled at him and promised teasingly, 'I'll try and eat more pizza and pasta, then!'

The following day, Bastian had overseen his father's welcome return from hospital into Dolores's care, with strict instructions that she wasn't to waste a moment in getting help if he was in any difficulty.

Alberto had been discharged because thankfully he'd taken a turn for the better. Was it the news about the baby and Bastian's marriage to Lily that had boosted his health? Even his medical team had been surprised at his progress, and had advised that as long as he adhered to their suggestions on diet and exercise, and took plenty of rest too, a full recovery was now anticipated.

At least that was one worry that had been eased from his shoulders, Bastian thought now, offering up a silent prayer of thanks.

Lily had insisted she still wanted to rent her house until they got married, but Bastian had told her he wouldn't dream of taking so much as a single euro from her. She was soon going to be his wife, and it would be his privilege to let her stay there until the wedding.

But when they were alone together he was wary of raising the topic of the wedding again in case it pushed her even further away from him. He had to tread carefully. He was wary of upsetting a pregnant woman.

And yet there was a side to his nature that didn't always lean towards being so understanding. He still bore a remnant of fury inside him because she hadn't answered her phone when he'd been trying to find her. She'd put him through the wringer that day, and he still didn't fully understand why.

A few days later, when they were both still walking on eggshells around each other, Lily came into the kitchen as he was preparing lunch for them both. He could easily have hired someone to come in and cook, but he'd got into the habit of going to her place at lunchtimes to make sure she ate something nutritious and to see for himself that she was doing okay.

He'd accepted the good-humoured banter that he'd got from his workers when he'd told them that she was pregnant but they were far from lacking in understanding. The majority of them were fathers themselves.

'Can I have a word?' she asked now, her tone sounding more serious than usual.

Standing at the marble counter, where he'd been slicing peppers, Bastian tensed before turning around to acknowledge her. She was wearing baggy jeans and a pale lemon sweater, but the practical clothing didn't detract one iota from Lily's natural sexiness. In fact as he studied her he sensed the inevitable stirrings of desire throb through him.

'What's up?'

Touching her hair, she pushed back a stray strand of gold that was brushing her cheek. Her big green eyes had the luminosity of dazzling emeralds, and Bastian knew that if he looked into them for too long he would be well and truly lost.

'I've decided that I *would* like to get married in your church after all,' she announced.

He breathed out a long, slow breath. All thought, all feeling, turned preternaturally still. 'What made you change your mind?'

'I realised that I was being selfish in not agreeing to get married there. You've already done so much for me and I can see that it means a lot to you. I've learned that family and tradition are very important to the people here.'

'They are indeed.'

'And, on that subject, I took your advice and asked my parents to come to the ceremony. My mum said they would. She told me that she and my dad are talking again and are working towards putting their past difficulties behind them. Anyway, that's all I wanted to say.'

She shrugged as though the decision had been a simple one and there was no need for elaboration. But Bastian wasn't going to let her off so easily.

Moving towards her, he caught hold of her slim upper arms and brought her closer to him. 'Do you really want to go through with the original arrangements or are you saying that just to placate me?'

'Why should I need to placate you? No, I mean what I say. Can we just leave it at that so I can get back to work?'

'And does this somewhat surprising decision mean that you'll be a little bit warmer towards me and not behave as though we're enemies instead of lovers?'

She gasped. 'I've never thought of you as my enemy, Bastian. How can you believe that for even a second? Is that perhaps how you view *me*?'

'Of course I don't.'

He wished he could *show* her what he

thought, rather than just tell her, but he knew he couldn't let his intense frustration get the better of him. For the first time in their relationship he promised himself he wouldn't let desire get in the way of proper communication.

Loosening his hold on her, he stepped aside. 'I have a question for you too. Why did you break off your call so abruptly that day when we were discussing the wedding? Had I said something to upset you?'

'Yes… I mean, no…'

She was twisting her hands together, and it seemed as though she was struggling to stay composed. Her plump lower lip was definitely bearing the brunt of things as her even white teeth chewed down on it.

'It just totally threw me when you said you'd meant the church wedding to be your gift to me and one that you'd hoped I would always cherish. I— That was the very *last* thing I expected you to say…especially when our relationship hasn't conformed to tradition in any way.'

His expression was gently mocking. 'You mean because it came about through our insatiable lust for each other instead of a so-called fairy-tale romance?'

'Yes… I suppose…'

'Do you think it means I think any less of you because we didn't get to know each other properly first?'

Her cheeks flushing, she said quickly, 'I didn't say that. *Any* woman would be moved by the declaration you made. I just wasn't expecting it. I ended the call because I needed some time to reflect and think about things more deeply, that's all. And, having done that, I've realised I *do* want our wedding to be conducted in the church. It's inspiring to me that your forebears got married there down the generations, and it seems only natural that you would want to do the same. Anyway, it suddenly just felt *right* to me.'

Rubbing his hand round his jaw, he felt secretly elated that Lily had reconsidered her decision and had attested to being moved by what he'd said. He was also touched that she'd had the courage to renew relations with her parents and invite them to the wedding.

There was now no doubt in his mind that his decision to marry her was absolutely the right one—whether she was having his baby or not. Not only was she beautiful and talented, but she had great sensitivity too. For her to realise that he had certain values and to respect them was no small thing.

'I'm glad you feel like that,' he said. 'Do you think we can both start to get on a little better now?'

'Of course. It's important for the baby to feel that his mother is happy, don't you think? And it won't help matters if we both continue to be on edge around each other.'

'How do you know we're having a boy?'

'Did I say that?'

'You did. You said it's important for the baby to feel that *his* mother is happy.'

Lily's porcelain-pale cheeks turned pink. 'It was just a figure of speech. It could just as easily be a girl.'

'Do you have a preference?'

'Not at all. I just want him or her to be healthy.'

'It goes without saying that I feel that way too. Now, shall we seal our new understanding with a kiss?'

Surprising him, she took the initiative and immediately closed the gap between them. Putting her hand against his cheek, she tentatively touched her lips to his.

Bastian grinned. 'I think you are seriously

out of practice, *l'affeto mio amore*. Let me remind you what a *real* kiss is…'

He took her mouth like a man who'd been denied sustenance for too long. As soon as he tasted her he was hungrily reminded of what he'd been missing. An avalanche of want and need descended on him and he yearned to touch her everywhere, to lose himself inside her knowing that she was what he'd long been waiting for…a woman who was generous-hearted and kind, who didn't hesitate to respond to her sensual nature in spite of being hurt and disappointed in the past, a woman who really *cared* about the important things in life like home and family.

As they stood together in the middle of the kitchen floor his hands eagerly started to explore her and her pliant body leaned naturally into his. Cupping the swell of her breasts, he noted excitedly that her nipples had already tightened in anticipation of his attention, and he avidly kissed the side of her neck.

But as he started to lift her sweater, to remove it and whatever other garments she had on underneath, Lily's hand firmly clamped down on his to stop him.

His dark eyes widened in surprise. 'What's wrong? Don't you want this?'

'You know I do. I *always* want you. That's the trouble. When I want you everything else goes out of my head—and that's not always so good. I'm trying to finish my book so I can send it to my publisher—the book you said I should write—and *you* have to finish preparing our lunch and get back to work. Sometimes we need to be sensible, Bastian.'

The fact that she was echoing what he'd thought previously—that they shouldn't let their desire for each other stop them from communicating properly and being pragmatic—didn't help right then. He was so desperate to have her that he doubted if even a bucket of iced water tipped over his head could cool him down. And Lily had added fuel to the fire when she'd told him how much she wanted him—that she *always* wanted him.

But she was right, of course.

It *was* important for her to get on with her book, and he *did* need to finish doing lunch and get back to work himself. His team were making good headway, preparing the land for the new olive groves, and he had to oversee

the procedure as well as lend a hand wherever it was needed. However, he couldn't help
protesting…

'Then answer me this. Why do you always
have to be so damn tempting? Even just the
scent of your body drives me wild!'

Her answer to that was to wriggle free and
hurry towards the stone arch that led into the
living room. 'Trust me. You'll thank me for
not giving in to you now because I'm sure
we can make up for it later. Whether it's tonight or tomorrow, the prospect will give you
something to look forward to.'

On her face was the most bewitchingly
sexy grin that would surely have the power to
tempt an avowed celibate. In spite of the gruff
protesting groan he released, he couldn't help
but smile.

They were waiting in the jeweller's, where
the furnishings and fittings were nothing less
than luxuriously opulent. Lily had had jitters
in her tummy from the moment Bastian had
guided her inside the building, and she sensed
they were not easily going to go away.

As they sat down on a grand purple velvet couch in the plush waiting room, clearly

concerned that she'd suddenly become too quiet, he asked, 'What's the matter? Are you nervous?'

'Of course I'm nervous. It's not every day a woman is invited to some fabulous jeweller's to have her wedding and engagement rings designed. At least not in *my* world.'

His eyes looked deeply into hers and he took her hand into his. 'This *is* your world now, Lily, and it's my privilege to do this for you. I want you to *enjoy* the experience. Not fear it.'

She felt the tiniest hint of a smile at the edges of her lips. 'Well, then, I will. The truth is, I feel I can do anything when you're by my side.'

This startling confession made the heat rise in his face—as if his very soul had just been bared to her. He was disorientated and dizzy, as if he'd just drunk a carafe of the strongest wine. The unexpected urge to say the words he'd once vowed he would never again say lightly was sorely testing him.

Thankfully, remembering he'd told her that theirs was to be a marriage of convenience, he shelved the impulse.

'Signor Carrera. My apologies for making you wait…'

Glancing up, Lily saw a handsome man in his mid to late forties enter the room. Gianni de Luca—the Carrera family's friend and personal jeweller—was dressed immaculately in a pristine charcoal-grey suit with a matching waistcoat and a maroon silk tie.

Bastian stood up to greet him and was immediately enveloped in a hug. 'It is so good to see you, my friend,' Gianni declared. 'It has been far too long.'

'Yes, it has. I'm sorry we had to cancel last time at such short notice. But we are here now.'

'Yes, you are.'

Lily had also got to her feet and stood waiting silently beside Bastian for the introductions to be made. For their visit today she was wearing a tailored navy blue jacket, a magnolia silk vest and white linen trousers. On her feet she wore plain navy pumps. Her make-up was, as usual, understated, but she had styled her hair a little differently. It was combed straight, with a parting on the side.

Just looking at her, Bastian felt his heart

beat faster and he was filled with pride. In his opinion no one could buy the kind of effortless class she exuded…for her, it was innate.

Sliding his arm around her waist, he said, 'Gianni, I'd like to introduce you to my fiancée. This is Lily—Lily Alexander'

'I am delighted to meet you, *signora.*' The designer dipped his head towards her in a polite bow. '*La tua bellezza e squisito*—your beauty is exquisite. How has my friend kept you a secret for so long?'

'I don't think he meant to hide me, *signor*. It just took him a little while to make up his mind about me.'

Amused, both men chuckled, and Bastian's possessive hold on her waist became a little firmer.

'You can see I will have my hands full with this one!' he joked.

'I wish I could be so lucky,' the jeweller commented. 'But now comes the important part—the purpose of your visit. I need to know what is your heart's desire in my making these rings for you, *signora*, and also for your husband-to-be? My creativity does not take full flight until I feel I know intimately what you hope for.'

'You can trust what he says, *tesoro*,' Bastian remarked, with a reassuring smile on his lips. 'Gianni's philosophy is never to disappoint. He will make to the letter the rings you have in mind and—more importantly—the rings that you hold in your heart.'

Hectic colour swept through her cheeks, as though he'd admitted knowing something she'd previously kept hidden. Bastian wondered what had discomfited her. All he knew was that he was becoming more and more fascinated by the prospect of getting to know her and, given time, of learning her most intimate secrets…

The last few hours had passed as though she were in some kind of fantastical dream, Lily thought. The two Italians had treated her as if she was royalty—as though even the most inconsequential thing she said was important.

Drinks and snacks had been brought to them at varying intervals, but she had mostly declined them. Anything that made her nervous always affected her stomach. But after talking through a few style variations she'd liked with Gianni, she'd been surprised to find that she'd felt more *excited* than nervous. Especially when he'd revealed that Bastian had requested the stone in her engagement ring to be a pure hand-cut diamond.

Her pulse had raced as fast as an athlete racing for the finishing line when Gianni had related this, and her glance had immediately sought her fiancé's. He'd given her one of his slow, sweet smiles in return and shrugged his shoulders.

This really was another world and she'd better get used to it. If it made him happy that she should take pleasure in his gift then so be it. She wouldn't again exhibit what he'd initially imagined to be ingratitude, like when she'd first declined his plans to marry in church.

Thoughts had then been turned to the design for his wedding ring and it had been decided upon. It would match hers, in yellow rolled gold, but of course in a much more masculine style.

By the time they'd finished Lily had been utterly exhausted. After bidding the jeweller a fond goodbye, they'd had dinner at a charming bijou restaurant in town and then headed for home.

Lily hadn't meant to fall asleep, but somehow, while Bastian was in the kitchen making her some hot chocolate, the impulse had been too hard to resist.

The trouble was the couch was ridiculously comfortable, and she'd felt so tired that she'd automatically rested her head against the cushions and dozed off.

The first thing she knew about it was when she woke to find him carrying her upstairs, his dark eyes gazing into hers.

'It's been a long day,' he said. 'I think we'll forget the hot chocolate for tonight and just get you into bed.'

'Yes, please...' she murmured, trustingly snuggling against his chest. And that was the last thing she remembered.

When she woke the next morning, to find the sun heralding a new day, she wondered what on earth had happened. It was disturbing enough to discover that a whole night had passed without her knowing, but then came another surprise.

She realised that beneath the covers, she was utterly naked.

Scrabbling to sit up, she drew the light duvet protectively around her body and tried hard to get her head straight. How on earth she couldn't have known that Bastian had undressed her when she knew his touches and his scent so intimately was beyond her.

More importantly, where was he now and had he spent the night with her?

Hurrying into the en-suite bathroom, she splashed some cold water on her face and brushed her teeth. Did *every* woman look as if she'd been dragged through a hedge backwards in the morning, or was it just her?

With a start, it came to her that it was probably nearer midday than early morning. And as for Bastian's whereabouts—he was probably already out, overseeing his workers in the fields. What on earth would he think of her, lying in bed this late?

Reaching for her robe, she hurriedly pulled it on.

The next instant a knock sounded at the door.

'Lily? Are you awake?' called a heart-stoppingly familiar voice.

'Just give me a minute, can you?'

Muttering under her breath, she dived into the bedroom and pulled out the drawer in the dressing table where she kept her underwear.

Completely ignoring her request, Bastian opened the door. 'What do you need a minute for?' he drawled.

'I—I want to get dressed.'

'Is that really necessary?'

His provocative reply hardly helped matters. Plus, he was wearing only jeans himself. His top half was bare, and that revealed the kind of arresting physique that came as a by-product of working on the land, displaying muscles that were noticeably hard and lean. There was not so much as an inch of fat on his body.

Looking at him now, Lily could hardly believe he was a businessman too. Most men would give their eye-teeth to have a body like his—and most women would fantasise about him long into the night, she was sure.

Giving her an intimate smile that she swore could a melt a glacier, he shoved a hand through his hair and dropped down onto the bed.

Completely flustered, she asked irritably, 'Why did you let me sleep in so late? A whole day has vanished and I wanted to get up early. Did you spend the night here with me?'

Grinning disarmingly, he replied, 'Do you

know what a blow it is to my ego that you have to ask me such a question? Are you saying you can't remember?'

'Well, *did* you?'

'You've dealt me another blow if you're still not sure.'

Pulling the robe a little more securely around her, Lily knew her cheeks must resemble twin flags of hot scarlet. 'Don't tease me. The last thing I remember is you carrying me up to bed and telling me we'd have to forget the hot chocolate. After that...' She reddened again. 'After that—*nothing.*'

'You have no need to fear, *tesoro*. As tempting as you are in the flesh, I am a man of honour. After talking to my father on the phone for a while—he sends you his best, by the way—and catching up with some other important calls, I spent the night in your spare room. I've just come to ask if you need anything.'

Thinking she could finally relax, knowing she hadn't been intimate with him without her knowledge, Lily met his glittering glance more confidently. She already knew that she could *more* than trust him not to take advantage.

'You're always asking me if I need anything.' With her voice a little husky, she murmured, 'But what about *you*, Bastian—what do *you* need?'

CHAPTER NINE

With her provocative question taunting him, Bastian's gaze alighted on her flushed face. Dry-mouthed, he answered, 'That's easy. There are two things I'd like. First, I could really use a back massage. It's hard on the muscles, digging over that land. And, second, while you're doing that I'd like you to take off your robe.'

She sucked in a breath and slowly let it out. 'Then come a bit closer and I'll see what I can do.'

Climbing onto the bed, she turned towards him. How could she refuse him when she'd still not delivered on her promise that he would have something to look forward to when she'd stopped him undressing her the other day? Besides, she needed to have him close again. Just the two of them with no distractions.

Obligingly, he moved to sit down with his back towards her and positioned his jeans-clad legs over the side of the bed. His whole body tensed in anticipation even before Lily took off her robe or touched him.

As things transpired, she didn't remove the garment straight away, but laid her hands on his skin and gently moved them round and up in circling motions. Initially not a lot of pressure was applied, but gradually her touches grew firmer, making him bite back the occasional groan. When she started to massage his shoulders—the place where he held most of his tension—he didn't hold back on his feelings and this time let loose a full-throated groan.

'I'm sorry if this hurts you, but I want to try and iron out some of the knots,' she explained, and the warm breath that drifted over him added to his tension rather than lessening it.

'Don't worry. I'll bear it. But I figure you've got to be a masochist to *enjoy* this kind of thing,' he declared wryly.

Right then, her skilful manipulations were giving him the most intense pleasure combined with pain that he'd ever experienced.

The temperature of his blood was already on simmer, and if Lily carried on like this for very much longer he'd turn around and strip off her robe himself.

The massage stopped suddenly. Scarcely daring to breathe, Bastian heard the rustle of her silken robe and sensed the cool satiny material briefly brushing against his flesh as she took it off.

'I think the least I can do is reward you for being so brave.'

His heart started to beat hard and fast. When he turned around Lily was kneeling on the bed, her arms by her sides. For the first time he saw her in all her beauty, her exquisite form unhindered by clothing. Her smooth, slightly rounded belly was revealed in its glory, also the pink-tipped roundness of her perfect bared breasts.

A thrill of fierce possession at the thought that the baby she was carrying was *his* lit up his insides like a firework display.

Joining her on the duvet, Bastian laid his hands on hips that were pleasingly curvy in the flesh and hungrily impelled her towards him. Taking her mouth first, he claimed her lips with a hard, hot kiss...a *sexy* wet-mouthed kiss…and his tongue duelled commandingly with hers.

Hearing her pleasured moan, he tipped her back onto the bed and sat astride her, his strong thighs imprisoning her until he could undo his belt and take down his jeans. To his surprise, Lily's eager hands reached his buckle first and skilfully undid it. When her fingers moved down to undo his zip his hand covered hers and helped guide her.

A moment later, as his gaze fell into her bewitching green eyes, he saw the unspoken invitation in her eyes. 'How do you do that?' he asked. 'I mean, stoke the desire in me to a furnace with just one look?'

'I think you should stop talking.'

His lover smiled, at the same time reaching towards him to help ease his waistband down over his hips. When she released him and encircled him with her hand Bastian's desire quickly reached fever-pitch. But he didn't take her straight away, like he'd done before.

Not even taking time to rid himself of his jeans, he kissed her on the mouth again, shamelessly goading her. Then he pushed her down onto the bed. Expertly guiding her silken thighs apart, he stroked his fingers over her most feminine place and teased her core. Feeling her delicious wetness, he started to explore her with his fingers.

With her beautiful hair tumbling over her shoulders, Lily moaned and threw her head back, and he knew that he wanted to pleasure her and take her to the ultimate moment of release even before he considered his own satisfaction.

He knew exactly when that moment arrived. She raised her hips and panted as though her pleasure was nigh on impossible to contain, and then she sank back into the bed, breathing hard. The expression on her face was one of sheer astonishment.

A few seconds later she breathed softly, 'I didn't know when you knocked on my door just now that you were going to take me to heaven…'

His lips edging into a smile, Bastian commented, 'Then perhaps you shouldn't have opened it?'

Before she could answer him he captured her lips. Releasing them, with no more delay, he unequivocally plunged inside her. Mindful of lying on her belly, he raised himself up, his biceps bulging powerfully as he took his own not inconsiderable weight.

He loved the way her expression responded to his attentions. Her features stayed outwardly calm, but her eyes were intense as she welcomed his body into hers, suggesting not the slightest resistance or doubt. If he'd had to describe her response he would have said that—trusting him—she surrendered naturally.

Owning to feeling a kind of satisfaction in an intimate union that he'd never felt before, he knew he was vastly enjoying giving her pleasure as well as taking his own. When his desire reached its zenith, consuming him with thrilling waves of carnal satisfaction, he released a full-throated cry and for a precious few moments gathered Lily into his arms.

Smiling up at him, she teased, 'That was *my* turn to take you to heaven, *amore…*'

Rolling over to lie by her side, he tenderly stroked back her hair and commented, 'If it were possible I would *never* leave this heavenly place I've found here with you, my angel.'

Her brow puckered a little. 'If I didn't know

better I'd think you were a secret romantic. *Are* you?'

'Only when I'm with you, beautiful.'

'Well...' She sighed. 'All's right with our world, then, isn't it?'

But again, even before the words left her lips, Lily knew her world couldn't possibly be right until Bastian told her that he loved her...

As soon as she entered the exquisite six-teenth-century church, she was suffused by an unexpected wave of guilt. Reflecting on why that should be, she quickly realised it must be due to the conditioning that people had been subject to down through the ages.

If Lily considered God at all, she didn't believe he had ever set out to punish people for so-called wrongdoing. She liked to think he was much more forgiving. Even so, she couldn't help smoothing her hand protectively over her belly as she sat down in one of the carved pews at the back.

Her baby had come from love—at least on *her* side—and that was what mattered, she told herself. All the same, the thought couldn't help but stir her emotions.

The fact was, even though he was always

eager to *make* love to her, Bastian had never actually *said* that he loved her. Even the other day, when she had instinctively turned the tables and asked him what *he* needed, the massage she'd given him had inevitably ended up with them being passionately intimate. And even though his words had been tender, he still hadn't told her the one thing she really wanted to hear.

Anyone knowing her story would probably ask what she was complaining about. She knew it would appear that she had everything a woman could dream of. After all, she was living in a beautiful place, in inspiring natural surroundings that enabled her to do the work she loved, and she was having a baby with the most incredible man she'd ever met.

They'd had an electrifying connection right from the start. The kind of connection that surely only happened to the lucky few. But not to have his love… Lily would always feel that she'd been denied the most important and essential thing of all.

After dabbing at her eyes, she returned her handkerchief to her pocket and endeavoured to focus on the awe-inspiring architecture that surrounded her. Feeling sorry for herself was utterly pointless. Better to focus on what was right in her life.

This was her second visit to Bastian's family church, and she was utterly charmed by its beauty and historical significance—but more importantly by how much it mattered to him.

In the past few days she'd learned more and more how considerate he was, and how he counted all the blessings in his life rather than just being thankful for the material ones. During their initial visit to the church he'd told her that he believed their coming baby was an incredible gift to them both and said he hoped she felt the same.

Of course she did, but she still had to pinch herself at the idea that all this good fortune was in any way *real*. She'd become so used to the feeling of waiting for the other shoe to drop—especially after her demoralising wedding night with her ex—that she almost *expected* things to go wrong.

But now, just when the urge to give in to her fears seemed almost too hard to resist the preternatural silence that surrounded her started to seep into her bones and have a profound effect. In the quiet and the stillness, for

almost the first time in her life, Lily attested
to feeling truly at peace.

As she breathed out a sigh the thought
came to her that maybe everything *was* going
to be all right after all.

An editor at the publishing house that com-
missioned Lily's illustrations, Kate Barrington, had wasted no time in getting back
to her. Lily had sent her the completed children's story she'd written, along with illustrations, and had been on tenterhooks ever since.

The woman's verdict was that it was just
what the children's market needed—'A fresh
voice that gently teaches valuable lessons as
well as having an important sense of fun.'

Lily was bowled over by her comments,
as well as being thrilled that they were interested in publishing the story.

In the meantime, now she was just over
three months pregnant, her waistline was in-
creasingly expanding. She'd had fittings for
her wedding dress, praying it wouldn't turn
out to be a colossal waste of money if she got
too big to wear it, but Bastian's response to
that observation had been to tease her.

'I can get a seamstress to let it out as much

as you need, sweetheart, so what's the problem? And no matter *how* big you get, Lily, you'll still be one hell of a sexy mama!'

After which he'd taken her in his arms and in very sexy Italian had incorrigibly whispered how much he wanted her.

But now she had another dilemma. Kate had invited her to London to discuss the book and have lunch. 'Why not take a couple of days off and also do some shopping?' she'd suggested.

Personally speaking, Lily couldn't think of anything *worse*. It was bad enough that she wouldn't see Bastian for what amounted to three whole days, when she included travelling there and back and the time needed to discuss the book, let alone dealing with the emotions that were bound to surface in the teeming city where previously everything had gone sour for her. But in the end, she decided she would go.

It was too good an opportunity to discuss her work and find out more about what the publishers were thinking of offering her and how they planned to publish her work. For instance, would they ask her to do another book? It would be a dream come true if they did. Wasn't that *always* what she'd wanted? To write her own stories and illustrate them instead of just illustrating others?

That evening, after they'd eaten, she decided to pluck up the courage to tell Bastian about her intended trip.

Accepting the glass of wine she offered him, he put it carefully down on the table and patted the couch next to him, indicating that she join him. For a long moment he didn't say anything, but his gaze suggested he was deep in thought.

'I sense that you want to tell me something,' he remarked.

Lily wasn't at all surprised he had tuned in to her.

'I do, as a matter of fact. I've been invited to go to London to discuss my book with an editor at the publishing house that employs me to do book illustrations.'

'You mean they're interested in buying it?'

'Yes…it seems they are.'

'When did you find out?'

'This morning.'

'And you didn't think of telling me earlier? You could have rung me on my mobile.'

She had a knot in the pit of her stomach

the size of a dinosaur egg hearing the dismay in his voice. 'I suppose I didn't say anything straight away because I knew I'd have to go to London. I'll probably be gone for about three days or so, and I didn't want you to worry…'

His hypnotic dark eyes narrowed. 'Is there any need for me to be concerned?'

'No, there isn't.'

'Well, it's my observation that you're a grown woman, Lily…not a child. Clearly you should keep this appointment.'

'I'm glad you agree.'

'In any case, I intend to accompany you.'

'You do?' She couldn't contain her surprise. It was the last thing she'd expected him to say.

'Of course. You're going to be the mother of my child and I want to ensure that you are safe.'

Although what he said was true, she was hurt and disappointed that his main priority seemed to be the baby. He didn't seem to be concerned about *her*…

'Of course I'll be safe,' she said testily. 'Have you forgotten that I lived and worked in London before I came to Italy?'

Bastian wasn't moved. 'Even so, it's a big

city, and people will be too concerned about themselves to consider a pregnant woman who's on her own.'

'I can't be the only pregnant woman in London!'

He heaved a sigh. 'Do you *enjoy* being deliberately difficult?'

Lily knew she wouldn't win this particular battle. She was already aware that she was trying his patience.

'I'm not being difficult. I only wanted to reassure you that I'll be perfectly all right.'

'Good. Then I will go and arrange our flights and a hotel. Can you tell me where your meeting is, exactly?'

Bastian hadn't liked it one bit that Lily wanted to attend her meeting alone. He had never felt he needed to be needed before, but that was what this relationship had done to him. He certainly didn't want to spend three days or more without her, and her announcement that she had to go to London had played on his insecurities. Especially because he knew that her ex still lived there.

What if they'd arranged to meet up? What if she still *loved* the man? More to the point, why hadn't she been more forthcoming in telling him about her past relationships? Was she trying to hide something?

His stomach churned sickeningly at the thought.

Endeavouring to get a grip on his emotions, he told himself that at least he now knew that he would be accompanying her. Feeling relieved, he was determined to focus on the positives of the trip.

The fact that Lily's publisher was interested in this new book was wonderful, but if memory served him right he hadn't even offered his congratulations. He would at some point have to show her that he was *more* than pleased for her.

When she'd first given him the news about London he'd straight away speculated on all the things that might go wrong, worrying about her and the baby and whether she would be too vulnerable in a city that would be swarming with people—everyone intent on pursuing their own business and not noticing if she happened to be in trouble.

Rightly or wrongly, he knew he couldn't let her do this by herself. Even though Bastian had talked to her many times about having more faith in her decision-making, he couldn't totally trust that she would be safe. So, to ensure her and the baby's safety, he was adamant he would make the trip with her.

Knowing that her enigmatic fiancé was waiting for her back at their hotel should have helped lessen Lily's nerves about her upcoming meeting, but in truth it didn't. It wasn't that Bastian hadn't been very forthcoming in wishing her luck, or in telling her that everything would go well, it was the fact that his over-protective behaviour had put her on edge.

She got the sense that he was more intent on making sure the baby was looked after than Lily, and that hardly reassured her. Add to that the fact that their personal irritations with each other had spilled over—both on the plane and during their arrival at the airport— she wasn't looking forward to the discussion about her book as much as she should have.

However, Kate Barrington was reassuringly charming and set her mind at rest. Radiating a confident professionalism that Lily couldn't help but admire, the woman was unfailingly warm and friendly.

From the moment she introduced herself in the reception area of a stylish London restaurant, she put Lily at her ease. And after ordering lunch from the menu, the women made easy and natural conversation right from the start.

Lily found herself relaxing more than she'd anticipated. However, the place was full of smartly dressed City types, and inevitably she couldn't help but remember what it had been like to be part of that world when she'd been married to Marc. She had never felt more on the outside of things than she had then.

But just as her all too familiar habit of not feeling quite good enough threatened to rear its head, she called to mind some of the reassuring advice Bastian had given her. Such as never to believe she was less deserving of good fortune and admiration than anyone else. That in fact she could hold her own with *anyone*. Not just because she was beautiful and talented, but because she was a genuinely good person and they were rare in this world. Who *wouldn't* want her company?

Her recent feelings of irritation towards him dissipating, she instead felt comforted by the very thought of him. As if to illustrate her feelings she laid her hand on her belly beneath the elegant gold-coloured tunic she wore and absently patted it.

'When is the baby due?'

Lily answered automatically. 'In about five months' time.'

'So he or she will be born in Italy?'

'That's right.'

'And the father...is he Italian?'

'Yes.'

'What's he like? Don't tell me he's absolutely *gorgeous*, with dark hair and big brown eyes, or I'll cry into my soup.'

Lily was still smiling at the remark when she momentarily glanced away and saw a small coterie of elegantly suited men being shown to a nearby table by a pretty waitress. She stared in surprise as she immediately picked out her ex-husband. Marc still texted her now and again, but they hadn't set eyes on each other since they'd divorced.

Seeing the expression on her face, Kate asked cheerfully, 'Seen someone you know?'

'My ex-husband.'

'Oh. Is that going to be awkward?'

Lily was already shaking her head. 'No... We're still friends.'

'So the divorce was amicable, then?'

'Yes, it was…' She grimaced. 'Though that doesn't mean it wasn't painful that things didn't work out as I'd hoped.'

'I don't doubt it. Most women are devastated when a relationship goes wrong. My sister went out with a guy in the same profession as that lot over there,' Kate commented disparagingly, jerking her head in the direction of Marc and his colleagues. 'He was just like them. He was quite full of himself and could be quite nasty at times. I'm not saying they're *all* like that, but thankfully she's with someone else now…someone in a caring profession—a nurse at Great Ormond Street Hospital. At least *his* heart is in the right place. He doesn't earn much money, but he loves her to bits and she says she's never been happier.'

'Well, on that note, why don't we drink a toast to all the *good* men in the world?' asked Lily.

But even as she spoke, she wondered if she'd ever be free of the humiliating memory of once being foolish enough to marry a man who preferred the opposite sex to hers and had knowingly denied her a wedding night?

CHAPTER TEN

BASTIAN HAD GONE out into the City ostensibly to get himself some lunch. But, although the choice of restaurants was myriad, Bastian had lost his appetite. He couldn't seem to get his mind off Lily. He hoped she was getting on all right with her new editor—hoped she wouldn't just take the first deal they offered in the belief that her efforts weren't worth more.

Wandering into a stylish café, he ordered an espresso and sat down in a window seat to drink it. He read the Italian newspaper he'd found and caught up on how his favourite football team was doing. But even that couldn't hold his attention.

The café was near Hyde Park, and half an hour later he went out into one of the most famous of London streets to hail a taxi.

Arriving at the smart Art Deco restaurant

where Lily's meeting was being held, he told himself it didn't matter that he was early. It was important that he saw for himself she was all right…

Lily had just left the ladies' room when she was surprisingly confronted by her ex-husband. Marc had obviously spotted her earlier, but had been too busy conversing with his colleagues to come over.

'Lily…what a lovely surprise!'

As though genuinely pleased to see her, he immediately planted a kiss on her cheek.

'I couldn't believe it when I looked across the room and saw you. What are you doing in London?'

'I'm having lunch with my editor.'

'So you've come over from Italy?'

She'd told him that she was moving there. 'That's right.'

'Well, if you don't mind my saying so, you're looking the picture of health. It must be doing you good, living there.'

'It is. I can honestly say I love it.'

'So, what have you been getting up to?'

'Well, quite a lot, actually. I'm pregnant and I'm getting married again.'

He seemed genuinely taken aback by this information and his face reddened slightly. 'You're expecting a baby?'

'I am.'

'No wonder you have such a bloom about you. Who's the lucky guy?'

'He's an olive grower. He and his family produce organic olive oil.'

'That's how he makes his living?'

'Yes…and he does very well at it.'

'Good for him…'

Not certain that he meant this at all, Lily was immediately defensive of Bastian. 'His family sells the oil all around the world and it's made their fortune.'

'How fortuitous for them.' He reddened again. 'So, when is the wedding to be?'

'In a couple of weeks' time.'

'And you love this guy?'

'Of course.'

She had no hesitation in admitting the fact, and realised that the difference in the feelings she had for both men was like night and day.

'So what's he like, this olive grower of yours?'

'He's generous, hard-working and…and rather wonderful, in fact.'

As soon as the words were out of her mouth Lily felt infused with joy that Bastian had come to London with her after all. Aware that she'd only wanted to make the trip on her own to show him she was quite capable of managing without him, she was glad he'd insisted to the contrary. Knowing he cared enough to want to accompany her, also that he intended to marry her, right then she felt the knowledge comfort her.

'Is he here with you?'

'You mean here at the restaurant?' Blushing, she shook her head. 'He's back at our hotel, waiting for me.'

Marc's expression was thoughtful. 'All I can say is that I just hope he knows how fortunate he is to have found you, Lily. I'm sure he must know that you're one of a kind.'

'And you, Marc? Are you any happier now?'

'Yes. I can honestly say I am.'

'Then life has changed for the better for both of us?'

Her companion turned silent for a moment. Then, sounding more than a little contrite, he said, 'I'm so sorry I hurt you, Lily. The truth is I was just too much of a coward to let you go. I feared I'd never find anyone who understood me like you did again. I wanted to have my cake and eat it, even though I knew I was stopping you from getting what you wanted.'

Finding it hard to deal with the tumult of emotion that was welling up inside her, she responded, 'I don't believe you *meant* to hurt me, Marc. We both sort of fell into getting married without much thought—no doubt because we just wanted to feel secure. We were comfortable together, so we chose what we thought was the easy option. I don't think there's any point in punishing ourselves by raking over old coals. Anyway, I'd better be getting back. My editor's probably wondering where on earth I've got to.'

Standing on tiptoes, she lightly brushed his cheek with her lips.

Having been advised by the affable Kate Barrington that Lily had been in the ladies' room for a little longer than expected, Bastian was immediately concerned that something was amiss. The fear that she might lose the baby was never far from his mind.

But as he stepped out into the elegant corridor that led to his destination his fury knew no bounds when he saw his fiancée reaching up to kiss a tall, elegant blond man. She clearly knew this man very well—and that led him to conclude that he must be the ex of whom Lily had told him so little.

It seemed that one of his greatest fears had been confirmed. Lily still had a thing for her ex-husband and they had arranged to meet up at the restaurant when she knew she would be there for her meeting.

'Lily! Would you mind explaining to me exactly what you're up to?'

With a look of surprise on her face, she quickly moved away from the other man. 'Bastian—how come you're so early? I told you I would ring you when I was done.'

'Then it's a good job I didn't listen to you, isn't it?' Raking his hand through his hair, he gave her a steely glance. But then he quickly moved his furious gaze across to her companion. 'You must be Lily's ex-husband.'

'What's it to you, may I ask?'

His perfectly manicured features flushing, the other man squared his shoulders. His arrogance infuriated Bastian even more.

Catching hold of Lily's hand, he drew her possessively against his side. 'What's it to me?' he echoed. 'Lily is having my baby and we're going to be married… Does that answer your question?'

'Believe it or not, I've just told her how pleased I am for her.'

'Have you really?' Moving nearer to the broker, his pristine tailored suit highlighting his superior physique and strength, Bastian demanded angrily, 'By all that's holy, what do you mean by arranging to meet her here? No doubt you know she's moved to Italy and is involved with someone else?'

Marc jutted his chin defensively. 'I didn't arrange to meet Lily here. Our seeing each other again is purely coincidental.'

Bastian schooled himself to take a deep breath before he replied, but his free hand was already clenching into a fist by his side. 'I don't believe for one moment that it is mere coincidence. But one thing I *do* know is that you should heed my warning to stay away from her.'

'I hear you. But surely it's up to Lily if she wants to see me again or not?'

Just before she spoke Bastian sensed the woman at his side trembling. Did she tremble because she wanted Marc more than she wanted him? he wondered. Why else had they met up? He didn't buy the story that their meeting was coincidental.

It was in those confusing, tormenting moments that he realised it wasn't just their baby he wanted. *It was Lily too.* He finally had to acknowledge that he wanted her for his own, whether she was having his baby or not. She had turned his ordered existence upside down and inside out since their very first explosive encounter. If she left him to go back to her ex-husband he didn't know what he would do. Would he even survive such a blow when she was the very air that he breathed to stay alive?

'First of all, Bastian, please don't refer to me as *her*,' she said tetchily. 'My name is Lily and I'm not invisible. And, secondly, it is pure chance that Marc and I happen to be here at the same time. However, I do agree that it's probably best that he doesn't get in touch with me again. I've started a new life now and our former relationship is well and truly over.'

Her green eyes swept over the other man.

'I've never said this to you before, Marc, but I was so unhappy when we were together— and you and I both know why. In conclusion,

I think it's best if we close the door on our friendship.'

'That's really what you want, is it?' Marc looked crestfallen.

Lily gripped tightly on to her lover's hand as she answered unequivocally, 'Yes, Marc. That's exactly what I want.'

On behalf of the publishers, Kate had offered Lily a good deal for her story—particularly, she said, because she'd already established herself as an illustrator.

The fact that she was going to be published as an author had helped Lily start to believe in her own talent. Her new contract proved she *could* write wonderful stories for children as well as illustrate them—stories that the public would want to buy. It wasn't just a long-held hope any more. It really was going to happen.

It had been an eventful day, what with signing her contract and Bastian unexpectedly showing up early and finding her in a potentially compromising situation with Marc, but it was by no means over yet.

Bastian had turned ominously quiet when they'd got into a taxi to take them back to their luxurious hotel, and she sensed that something disagreeable was brewing. Was he still angry about finding her in the corridor with Marc? But was it *her* fault that he had taken it upon himself to turn up at the restaurant to collect her earlier than they'd arranged?

'You'd better tell me what's on your mind, don't you think? I can tell you're not very happy,' she said.

Turning his unflinching dark gaze towards her, he returned, 'Did you arrange to meet up with your ex before I said I was coming with you?'

Lily knew she must have turned pale. 'Of course I didn't. I've already told you that it was a chance encounter. I didn't have a clue he would be there. I was just as surprised to see him as you were.'

'Is that the truth?'

'Why do you doubt me? You must have been able to tell that there's no attraction between us whatsoever.'

'Then why did you marry him?'

She sighed. 'Didn't I already tell you that?'

'You said something about your friend recommending him, and not wanting to be alone, but that doesn't tell me very much, Lily. I'd like to hear the full story. We need to talk about this some more. But not here. Right now I want to make the most of our trip and take you shopping.'

'Shopping for what?'

'For you and the baby.'

'But I don't need anything.'

Quirking an eyebrow, he commented, 'What about our baby? Do you expect him to stay naked? He's going to need clothes, blankets and other necessary items...' Leaning towards the cabbie and opening the small window that separated them, he instructed, 'Take us to Harrods, please!'

Just before they arrived at the famous store, Bastian informed Lily that he'd arranged for them to have a personal shopper—and that Lily should take advantage of the opportunity. Neither should she be shy in letting them know her personal preferences.

And, although she started out feeling a little awkward, she soon started to get the hang of things and began to enjoy herself. As they started to pick out clothing created by the best designers, and various other essential items for their baby, Bastian clearly started to enjoy himself too. She saw that he loved to talk about their baby with anyone who cared to listen, and there were a lot of appreciative women wherever they went, happily giving their opinions when he asked them.

She couldn't deny he'd worked his magic on her too. They'd chosen a veritable trunkful of stuff, which he'd arranged to have delivered to their Italian home, and it was then, with a twinkle in his eye, that he teasingly told her that it was her turn.

'What do you mean? I told you I don't need anything.'

'It's true that you don't *need* anything to make you look beautiful, Lily, but as the man in your life it's my privilege to select clothing that enhances your beauty, is it not?'

All but quaking inside at the idea of Bastian choosing clothes for her, she gave him a nervous smile...

They finished their day by visiting the Shard, and they couldn't have ended it more perfectly than by visiting the champagne bar on the fifty-second floor for cocktails and canapés and to admire the breathtaking views of the skyline. This was the city Lily had grown up in, but now she saw it with the eyes of an appreciative tourist and was proud as punch to see it like this for the first time with her handsome fiancé.

Before they left Bastian toasted their upcoming marriage with a champagne cocktail and kissed her avidly on the lips—just as she'd expect any man in love to toast his bride. Only she was still tormented by the idea that he didn't love her at all. That he was only marrying her because she was having his baby.

Lily was upstairs, unpacking her suitcase, and even now that they were back at Lily's small stone house Bastian could hardly settle to anything. That old fear of his—that fear of losing someone important to him—had inevitably surfaced. Losing his mother and then Marissa had seen to that, and if he cared too much about Lily it would be all the more painful if he should lose *her*. He might know without a doubt that he wanted her in his life, but after seeing her with Marc his feelings were running riot.

'Bastian.'

Suddenly appearing halfway down the stairs, she halted to glance over at him.

'I thought my unpacking could wait. There's something I want to tell you about.'

Did she want to confess that she regretted parting company with her ex?

Having been sitting restlessly on the couch, he got to his feet even as his gaze examined her hungrily. She'd changed into loose-fitting linen trousers and a white shirt, and had freed her pretty hair from its top-knot. Silken strands of gold glided gracefully down over shoulders. Silently he acknowledged how much he loved that look. The woman knew no artifice. She was simply always just herself.

The thought flashed through his mind that his mother would have adored her.

'Then why don't you come over here and sit down?' he invited.

Not needing a second bidding, she complied, waiting for him to resume his place before dropping down beside him. Wanting to hold her hand, he saw that they were both folded in her lap. For the first time he noticed that her face was flushed and serious.

For a few disconcerting seconds Bastian's stomach clenched. Then, 'What is it?'

'You said you wanted to hear the full story about Marc…'

He took an unsteady breath.

'Anyway…' Coiling some hair round her ear, she went on. 'Seeing him again made me determined to tell you the truth about him and our time together.'

'What do you mean by that? Are you going to tell me you've realised that it's *him* you want and not me?'

Her expression was genuinely shocked. 'How could you even *think* such a thing? Does what we've shared and the fact that we're having a baby mean nothing to you? Do you think that all along I've been *pretending* that I want to be with you?'

Shaking his head, he felt his heart sink like a stone. 'Right now I don't know what to think.'

Lily's gaze was intense. 'I want to tell you about Marc because you and I are about to get married, Bastian, and I don't want anything detrimental from my past hanging over me. I want to clear the air. I want you to know the full story of our relationship.'

'You'd better tell me, then.'

Clearing her throat, she twisted her hands together.

'I was twenty-six when I met him, and up until then I hadn't had even *one* proper relationship. I'd steered clear because I was wary of commitment. I didn't exactly have a good example from my parents, since they were always arguing and unhappy, and I didn't want to be in a similar relationship. Marc said he was attracted to me right from the start and, encouraged by my friend whose husband worked with him, I thought, *Why not go on a few dates and get to know him?* I'd been on my own for a long time, and when I wasn't illustrating books I was faced with the fact that I had no one in my life to help me enjoy it...

'Well, to cut a long story short, I started to enjoy his company. He was very good to me, and he knew how to cheer me up when I was down. I began to look forward to our dates, and when he asked me to marry him I thought it would be a good idea. At least I wouldn't be alone any more, and I'd have his support when I needed it as he would have mine. We went ahead and married. But then I found out something that I hadn't expected, and my hopes for a better future disintegrated before my eyes.'

'Was he cheating on you? Seeing someone else?'

Lily shrugged, and her silken hair unravelled from behind her ear and fell across her cheek.

'I don't know about that, but it's what he revealed to me on our wedding night that made our union destined to fail. Marc is gay. He's interested in *men*—not women.'

For what seemed like a long time words deserted Bastian. Of all the things he might have imagined, that hadn't even remotely entered his head.

Unable to sit still, he got up to pace the floor for a few seconds. Then, spearing a hand through his thick dark hair, he stopped in front of his companion and angrily shook his head.

'What the *hell* was he playing at? You mean to tell me he left it until you were married and on your wedding night to reveal this?'

'Yes, he did.'

Briefly he saw a disconsolate flash of pain cross the incandescent green irises.

'At the time I was truly shocked that he could be so selfish and marry me regardless.

But afterwards I felt like I'd betrayed *myself* for not listening to my intuition.'

'You mean you suspected the truth about his preferences earlier on?'

She nodded. 'I did. But I convinced myself I was just imagining it.'

'You weren't to blame. It's clear that he knew what he was doing when he tricked you into marrying him. He took appalling advantage of you. You should have rung the police and reported him straight away!'

Her glance was perplexed. 'How would *that* have helped? I can just hear their question now: *Did he coerce or threaten you into marrying him?* I'd have had to say no. I walked into it with my eyes wide open.'

Now it was her turn to shake her head.

'After the wedding night that didn't happen he made me a deal. He said that if I stayed and acted like a devoted wife—accompanied him to corporate dinners and made out that I supported his drive for success—he would be more likely to get promotions than if he was single, because the powers-that-be were surprisingly old-fashioned in their views. In turn he would support me financially. I had nowhere else to go, so what else could I do but accept his offer? I'd given up my flat-share and burnt all my bridges. I knew if I stayed with him that at least I'd have a base from which to work.'

'And so you stayed with him for nearly a year after his revelation?'

Bastian knew Lily must hear the disappointment in his tone because he saw her flinch.

'I'm not proud of that. Can you imagine how humiliating it was for me? Living with a man who didn't desire me and who had used my situation to better his own? But the fact was he knew his behaviour had hurt me and he tried to make things more bearable in any way he could.'

'How? By giving you nice things and impressing you with what his money could buy?'

She made a sound of distress, feeling as if she might die of pain and embarrassment right there.

'Do you really think I could be that shallow, Bastian?'

Swallowing hard, he knew his glance was fierce. 'No, I don't. But it makes me mad when I think of what that man must have put you through.'

'Anyway, I knew what I had to do. I came up with a plan to free myself. Along with the payments I received for my illustrations, I put some of the money he insisted on giving me for housekeeping and clothes into a savings account, with a view to moving abroad as soon as I could. I thought I would put my foolish mistake behind me and start over again somewhere new. Even then I was thinking about going to Italy…'

'So you told him you wanted a divorce?'

'Strangely enough, he beat me to it. He'd met someone, you see, and he told me it was serious. He wanted the guy to move in with him and said he was quite happy to bring our arrangement to an end. He offered to make me a settlement but I refused. I'd saved enough to support myself for a while, and I didn't want to be beholden to him in any way. However, at the last minute he insisted on writing me a cheque—to tide me over, he said, until I got back on my feet.'

She stood up, giving Bastian a forlorn glance that he didn't immediately understand.

'I'm sure you must think I'm an idiot for not taking him for all I could get. But…'

The beseeching look in her eyes nearly

undid him. And then he realised why she seemed so sad. Her next words confirmed it.

'But I'm just not like that. I can't be something I'm not, and I won't be cruel to someone just because they've hurt me. You probably think I'm too soft-hearted for my own good, and no doubt you're right.'

'You're making a lot of assumptions about what I think, Lily. None of which are true. I like and accept you just the way you are. If you were any different, it's likely we wouldn't be together.'

Reaching the end of his declaration, he didn't hesitate to take her into his arms. Gazing down into the moist emerald eyes that stared back at him, he tenderly smoothed back her hair and smiled.

'From what you've said I can tell that the man must have been conflicted—although that doesn't mean he should have done what he did. I'm glad I told him to stay away from you. But he's your past, *tesoro*, and I am your present—and, I trust, your future. Forget him. He was nothing more than a passing black cloud on a sunny day.'

'How do you have the innate ability to

make me believe that everything will be all right?' she murmured.

'I have it because I care about you, and I don't want our baby's mother to doubt herself.'

'I see. Then I'll make sure to try and be more confident when the baby comes.'

'*Trying* suggests effort, Lily. You don't have to be any different from who you are right now. You just need to forgive yourself for what you judge to be your mistakes. That will help you more than anything.'

'Hmm… Well, on that note, I think it's time for me to go upstairs and finish my unpacking.'

She deftly extricated herself from his embrace and before he could stop her moved nimbly up the stairs. In a few short seconds she'd disappeared into the bedroom.

Her revelations about her marriage to Marc had left Bastian reeling. Was he at fault in persuading her to marry *him* when she might not want that at all? He hoped that wasn't the case.

Relieved that at least she'd told him about life with her ex at last, Bastian was gratified that he could now focus on their wedding without any more suspicions that she might go back to the man.

She was 'fashionably late', as he'd heard a couple of guests in the congregation murmur.

Bastian was beginning to despise the phrase. 'Fashionably' should be replaced with *torturously*, as far as he was concerned.

His hand slid down the back of his stiffened shirt collar to loosen it. Even in the cool confines of the stone church it was surely as hot as Hades?

'It will be all right son,' his father reassured him smilingly—looking especially handsome today in an impressive tuxedo, and still recovering well from his heart scare. 'I'm sure it's just that her mother and her bridesmaids want to make sure she looks perfect for her special day.'

'Lily *always* looks perfect.'

'I agree,' Alberto replied. 'But you know how women like to fuss.'

Lowering his voice, Bastian said fervently, 'She's not just *any* woman…she's my heart and my soul-mate.'

The older man wiped some moisture from

his eyes. 'That's just the way I felt about your mother all those years ago...'

His son was squeezing his hand in empathy when the classical guitarist positioned at the front of the church started to play the opening chords of the bride's processional music. The notes rang out as crisp and clear as crystal in the vaulted church.

Father and son turned together. And as he set eyes on his bride in her wedding finery for the very first time Bastian gasped under his breath. The intensity of his feelings for this exquisite woman could only be described by his heart and not his head, he knew. Yet her exclusively designed off-the-shoulder gown in elegant taupe and white silk organza rendered her as lovely as a fairy princess from a mythical tale.

The sweeping skirt barely hinted at her condition, but it didn't matter to him one iota what people might think about it. He was certain of one thing: every man in the church must secretly envy his good fortune.

At the wedding breakfast afterwards he would bid his guests to raise their glasses to the most beautiful and gracious woman in the world: his *wife*, Lily Carrera.

CHAPTER ELEVEN

THEY DIDN'T HAVE their honeymoon immediately, because they couldn't decide where they wanted to go.

Lily had professed that she didn't mind where they went—it was the company that was important, not the scenery. But it was important to *him*. They might not have started off in the traditional way, but it was important to get this right. He wanted Lily to have the perfect honeymoon-—the one she'd so obviously missed out on the first time round.

Though he'd come to accept that Lily's feelings for her ex were dead and buried, Bastian still felt great shock and sadness for what she'd been through. He wanted to make sure that *their* marriage started out in the best way possible, in order to fully erase the pain of the past from Lily's consciousness.

In the end he told Lily to leave the destination to him. The idea had suddenly come to him to book them into a luxurious hotel he knew that was discreet and comfortable and where they wouldn't be disturbed. The hotel was about six miles from the Adriatic Coast, and it was highly regarded by his wealthy compatriots. Its menu and wine list were superb, and it had every facility even the most discerning client could desire.

Satisfied with these arrangements, he was just thinking about collecting Lily from the rental house, where she still preferred to work on her illustrations and stories, when someone rapped on the front door.

His stomach somersaulted. Had Lily decided to turn up unannounced and surprise him? The pleasure the thought gave him couldn't be measured.

But when he opened the door it wasn't his beautiful elfin wife who stood there, but an attractive woman of around thirty or so, with fashionably cut chestnut hair and a face that was strangely familiar.

At the same time as her crimson lips formed a hesitant smile he registered with shock that it was *Marissa*!

'Bastian! I was hoping I'd find you here. I

asked a couple of locals in town who know you, and they told me you had a place up here in the hills. Then I remembered how you'd always said that one day you were going to build a house here. What was that name you were going to call it? Can you remind me?'

Her words had come out in a hurried gush, and he sensed that she was unusually nervous.

Over a suddenly dry throat he managed a reply of sorts. 'I didn't expect to see you ever again, Marissa. I'd heard rumours that you'd moved to America. What brings you here?'

'Yes, I did move to the States. But I came back to revisit my past, and to remind myself of a time when I was much happier.'

There was a telling break in her voice and her dark eyes didn't disguise her emotion. Even so, Bastian couldn't help but feel it was all an act. They had a turbulent history together and he hadn't forgotten how she could be.

'Can I come in for a few minutes?' she asked.

'I don't think that would be a good idea, do you?'

As soon as the question was out of his mouth he knew he shouldn't have asked her.

'*Please*, Bastian.'

All his instincts urged him to say no. But being with Lily had to some degree softened his nature, and made him more apt to be forgiving than he'd used to be. After all, what was the point in bearing a grudge any more? He and this brunette had both been so young back then—surely they were no longer the same people? In particular, he hoped that the unexpected twists and turns and the vagaries of life would have helped his ex-girlfriend to grow up at last, whichever way her path had taken her.

'Okay…but it can't be for very long,' he answered. 'I have to see someone important.'

Holding the door wide for her to enter, he watched as she stepped into the hall and—as was her habit of old—deposited her indubitably impractical high-heeled sandals on the mat.

Marissa had never been much of a walker. and if it was a choice between following fashion or being practical, fashion won out every time.

Endeavouring to set his bittersweet memories of the past firmly aside, Bastian squared his shoulders, closed the door and guided her into the living room.

* * *

Lily was just loading the washing machine in her rented home with some of the clothing she wanted to take on honeymoon when there was a definite sensation of the baby moving in her belly. If she'd had to describe it she'd have said it felt as if it were practising acrobatics!

Breathing out a wondering gasp, she laid her palm against her tightened abdomen and felt the infant do a couple more turns. Nothing could have prepared her for the experience. It was just incredible.

There was no doubt in her mind that she should drive up to Buona Stella and tell Bastian about the occurrence immediately.

Deciding not to tell him she was on her way, she thought she would instead surprise him…

Excitement sustained her spirits during the drive there, but her buoyant mood immediately fled when she arrived and saw the vehicle that was parked outside the house. She wondered who the flashy red sports car belonged to.

Chewing worriedly on her lip, she parked her small and decidedly *non*-flashy little car quite a bit further away from the house, near a bank of tall cypress trees, and turned off the ignition. It disturbed her much more than she liked, seeing the other vehicle there.

Drawing in a steadying breath, she got out of the car and walked back to the house. Nothing moved in the still, sultry air as she crept up to the nearest window and stole a peek inside.

Just when she'd decided to go round the back and see if Bastian was with his guest in the kitchen, she saw her husband enter the living room with an attractive dark-haired woman. The look on both their faces was intense. Even as Lily's stunned gaze drank in the scene the woman turned towards Bastian and, without the slightest preamble, put her arms round his neck and kissed him passionately.

Everything inside Lily suddenly went terrifyingly still, and her ability to think at all utterly fled. As her heart started to thud heavily every nerve and sinew she possessed felt as if it was crying out in pain. *Please God, he can't be having an affair, can he?*

But even as the devastating idea entered her mind she was turning away from the scene. She tore back down the hill to her car and started to drive away too fast, scalding tears streaming down her face at the realisation that the man she loved was cheating on her.

Inside the house, Bastian had straight away disengaged himself from the distasteful woman who'd so unceremoniously grabbed him and kissed him. With his face clenching in annoyance, and without the remotest suggestion of politeness, he set Marissa aside as though she was something contagious.

'Don't touch me ever again,' he warned her, stepping away from her.

'Why? Is it because you're scared you might want me again? I'll bet your new woman doesn't satisfy you like I can.'

'My "new woman" is my wife, and she is a hundred times more woman than you can *ever* be, Marissa—and far more beautiful. I feel sorry for you that you can so easily delude yourself.'

Beyond furious, Marissa let loose a passionate invective, shouting that she couldn't believe he'd be so stupid as to rebuff her attentions. Just *who* did he think he was?

Following another heated exchange, she turned on her heel and stomped out through the front door to her ostentatious motor car.

It wasn't long before the vehicle sped noisily down the hill, and Bastian attested to being well and truly happy to see the back of her. But, truth to tell, the volatile confrontation had disturbed him. Seeing the woman again had painfully brought back the unpleasantness of their association. Like a tide that returned the detritus people had discarded into the sea to the shore. And treasure *definitely* didn't follow in her wake…

He was grateful that Lily hadn't seen their altercation in the house. It would have made her doubt everything that he'd told her—that he wasn't a man who would cheat on the woman in his life, that he had too much integrity for that. If she knew that Marissa had visited him she might believe that Bastian had *invited* her, and that would hardly put him in a very good light. She might even start to think he still held a candle for her after all these years, when nothing could be further from the truth.

He'd been mulling things over for far longer than he'd realised, and so it was much, *much* later when he got to Lily's place. Dusk had turned to night, but the warm, fragrant air was no less sultry.

When she opened the door to him, her glance was distinctly cagey.

'Hi,' she said, sounding as if it barely mattered if he was there or not.

Frowning, Bastian followed her into the living room. 'I'm sorry I'm so late. I had some business to take care of.'

'Was it to do with work?'

'Yes,' he replied, hoping his excruciating discomfort at telling this lie wouldn't betray him.

'That's tough when you thought you'd be getting some time off today. Can I get you a coffee?' she added, already making her way to the kitchen, even before he sat down.

'No, thanks,' he murmured, noting that her pale hair was still damp from a shower and that she was wearing a scooped-neck green shift dress with pearl buttons that he hadn't seen before. 'I'd much prefer it if you just came and sat down.'

'All right.'

It worried him that she sounded so calm. So much so that he'd almost have preferred it if she'd ranted and raved at him and accused him of being up to no good because he hadn't come to get her sooner. At least then he'd know what she was thinking and be able to reassure her.

She carefully lowered herself into an armchair. In spite of having invited her to sit down, Bastian remained standing. 'I can see that something is troubling you,' he started, 'and don't tell me it's nothing because I won't believe you.'

After briefly drawing in a deep breath, for once Lily had no hesitation in answering him. Her hurt and disappointment that he'd blatantly withheld the truth about his visit from the woman in the red car couldn't be contained.

'Okay… I'll tell you what's troubling me. I'm furious that you lied to me. Who was that woman in the red car visiting you and why did you try and hide the fact from me?'

'You came to the house earlier and saw her?' His face was stunned.

'Yes. I parked down the road away from the house when I saw the car, because I knew you must have visitors. I didn't want to interrupt anything important, so I thought I'd wait until they left before coming in. Anyway, I got worried when you didn't come out, and I stole a look in at the window to see if I could see you. I saw much more than I bargained for. I saw the brunette who was with you.' After pausing for a moment, she suddenly burst out, 'More than that, I saw her passionately kissing you. Is she your lover, Bastian?'

'No, of course she isn't… Is that what you think?' Inside, he felt his heart drumming hard.

'What else am I supposed to think when I see you in the arms of a strange woman only days after you made vows in front of all your friends and family?'

'If you saw that, then you must also have seen me push her away.'

'I didn't. I wanted to get away from the scene as fast as possible. Who *was* she, Bastian? And why would she take such a liberty if you weren't already intimate?'

'Her name is Marissa,' he announced, dropping his hands down to his hips and hooking his thumbs through his belt loops. When Lily didn't comment, he continued, 'Remember I told you that I was once engaged?'

'You mean she's the woman who cheated on you?'

His intense dark eyes scrutinised her features closely, trying to determine if she really believed he was having an affair.

'That's right. She's been living in America. Her second marriage recently broke down and she's come back to Italy to visit her old home and remind herself of what she left behind.'

He blew out a disparaging breath and a coil of rich dark hair brushed against his forehead.

'Meaning *you*?'

'Not only me…she was visiting her family too.'

'So what did you say to her?'

'I told her that I'd just got married.'

'Then why did she kiss you?'

'Because one of her more dislikeable traits is that she's apt to be jealous…spiteful too. She can't bear the thought that there's somebody in the world who doesn't want her.'

'How do you know she won't try to get you back again?'

'Whether she does or she doesn't, she'll be wasting her time.'

Lily was aching for him to say that he loved her, that he wasn't and would never be interested in any other woman again. But he didn't and so, feeling unsure and vulnerable, she spoke without thinking.

'This marriage isn't going to work out as I hoped it would, Bastian. More than anything I have to trust the man I marry, and right now… I don't trust you. So I'll pack my things and stay in a hotel for a while, until I can think a bit more clearly about all this.'

'You're really saying that you don't trust me?' He looked at her, aghast.

Sorrowfully, she nodded. 'Let's not make this any worse than it is already. I'll stay in touch with you, but I don't want to see you again until I've decided what to do.'

'Now you're being ridiculous—'

With a lump in her throat, Lily glanced at him disconsolately. 'No, I'm not. I'm just being sensible for once.'

Getting to her feet, she turned towards the stairs.

'But you're saying you're going to take my child away from me…do you know what that will do to me?'

For a moment his eyes were wild with distress, and that demonstrated to her just what it meant to him to become a father. But right then she had to steel herself against how *he* felt and put herself first.

'I'm going upstairs to pack some things and then I'm going to a hotel. Don't worry, Bastian. I'll phone and let you know where I am. Look…perhaps we should meet up again tomorrow, when we're both feeling a bit more clear-headed, and we can calmly discuss what we're going to do.'

'Tell me now, Lily. Are you saying you want us to break up?'

'I'm afraid it might have to be that way.'

'But you can't just leave and take my baby away… I won't let you!'

Shockingly, he grabbed her arm and yanked her towards him, his handsome face etched with desperation.

Distressed by his outburst, with her heart feeling fit to burst, she said, as calmly as she could manage, 'Let me go, Bastian.'

He hung on to her for a few seconds more, looking as though he hated every moment of what was happening. Then reluctantly he released her.

Without so much as a backward glance at the man she was leaving behind, Lily hurried upstairs…

* * *

'I can't believe she's gone.'

Bastian sat at his father's kitchen table, drowning his sorrows in a glass of brandy. Just saying the words he'd hoped never to hear himself say made him feel sick to his stomach. But he'd watched Lily take her suitcase out to the car, feeling too frozen to offer to help.

And why should he have provided the means to help her walk away from him? he reasoned. It near killed him that she didn't trust him any more. She'd said once that he had an innate ability to make her feel that everything was going to be all right, but today he'd learned that that was a *lie*.

Sitting opposite him, Alberto thoughtfully rubbed his hand around his beard. 'What happened, son? Why did she leave?'

Bastian took another generous swig of the spirit and felt it burn a fiery trail down into his stomach. His gaze distressed, he murmured, 'She thought I was cheating on her with Marissa.'

'Marissa? What in Hades has *that* woman got to do with anything?'

'Don't you know? She's back to visit her family.'

'You mean you saw her?'

'She called at my house and Lily looked through the window and saw her as she tried to kiss me.'

'What? I can hardly believe what I'm hearing. But one thing I *do* know: that woman is nothing but trouble…always was and always will be. I hope you told her straight where to go?'

Slamming down his glass on the table, Bastian got dazedly to his feet. 'I did, but it's too late, Dad. The damage is done. I'm destroyed without Lily—you know I am. I left it too long to tell her how much she means to me and now she thinks I'm nothing but a lousy cheat.'

'If that's true, then you have to put things right.'

'How? How do I do that when I've hurt her so badly?'

'Sit down again, son, and we'll talk about it. And before you do anything else put that brandy away. You should be stone-cold sober when you go to her and beg her forgiveness. And I mean *beg*—because you'll never find another woman like Lily. Be honest with her— tell her what you told me: that she's the love of your life and that's why you married her.'

* * *

Lily had never known just how lonely hotel rooms could be until she was shown into this one, with the covers on the single bed invitingly turned down and the chambermaid carefully shutting the door behind her.

Lily sensed her eyes filling with tears even as the maid wished her a *buona notte*. Over and over again in her mind she replayed that distressing scene when Bastian had cried out, *'You can't take my baby away from me!'* and she'd realised he could bear losing *her*, but not his child.

The agonising knowledge had made her know right then that she had to leave—that their relationship had been based purely on passion, but not on love. And it was his love that she craved most of all.

Unable to help herself, she turned her thoughts to the events of that afternoon. Had Bastian been telling her the truth about not having an affair with the sultry Marissa? Had she been too hasty in saying she didn't trust him any more? Probably not...

The truth was she just couldn't face the facts because once again her hopes of happiness with a man had blown up in her face. When would she ever learn?

Right then, as if the baby sensed her unhappiness, she felt it move with some force in her womb. Feeling slightly sick, Lily dropped down onto the bed behind her and as gently as she could rubbed her abdomen in a comforting circular motion.

'I'm so sorry, baby,' she whispered hoarsely. 'Mummy will be all right. She's just had a little tiff with your daddy and is feeling sorry for herself.'

But as soon as she'd finished saying the words she covered her face with her hands and once again allowed grief and regret to overwhelm her.

'We have to talk.'

Lily heard her husband's gruff-voiced tone at the other end of her mobile phone next morning with renewed trepidation. If she could have turned back time and made everything as it had been before she'd seen that woman's car parked outside Buena Stella, she would have done it. Now she both longed to hear Bastian's voice and feared what he might say to her after their row last night.

Afraid that she might buckle, and give in to demands that weren't in her best interests, she knew she had to be strong. 'Right now? On the phone?'

She heard him inhale a deep breath, then he replied, 'No. I would much prefer us to meet and talk face to face. Are you willing to do that?'

'If you can be reasonable.'

'You don't think I can?'

Lily sighed. 'There's a lot at stake here and I have to put my welfare and the baby's first.'

'So you think that *my* feelings about all this are inconsequential?'

He was angry—that much was clear—and she didn't want to add fuel to the fire by arguing with him any more, she thought. They both had to stay as calm as they could if they were to resolve anything.

'Where do you want us to meet?'

'At the rental house—it's a lot nearer for you to get to.'

'Then I'll see you there in about an hour,'

'Suits me.' And then, as if he had to have the last word, the Italian murmured, 'And don't be late.'

* * *

The weather report had promised another scorching day and Lily was already feeling uncomfortably hot. But she suspected the perspiration that trickled down the back of her neck was less about the heat of the day and more about being anxious over seeing her new husband again after the upsetting scene they'd had yesterday.

Lily had thought she'd be the first to arrive, but Bastian had beaten her to it. She was aware that he still had a key, and it was he who opened the door to the charming house he'd agreed she could use as her home office now they were married.

The realisation that they might be about to break up made her feel unhappy and desolate. It didn't help that Bastian was looking especially gorgeous today, whilst in contrast she was feeling particularly frumpy and unattractive in a smocked green dress and was devoid of make-up. She could have used some powder and paint to aid her confidence, but the truth was she didn't feel confident in any way. Instead she felt utterly wretched.

He started the conversation. 'Can I get you a cold drink?'

'No, thanks. I'd prefer it if we just got down to making some plans.'

She fiddled with her hair as she sat, trying not to let her gaze linger on the handsome carved face in front of her as he dropped down to sit on the sofa opposite. How was she going to bear not ever sharing a bed with him again?

'About Marissa…'

Lily's eyes immediately widened. 'What about Marissa?'

'I never told you this before, but she put me through hell when we were together,' he confessed. 'She led me a merry dance with all her lies and deception. Dumb of me, I know, but I thought I could help her change for the better. She only got worse. She was a serial flirt and she couldn't resist getting as much male attention as she could. I shouldn't have been surprised when I walked in on her in bed with somebody else. It sickened me, and for a long time I blamed myself. Why didn't I act on my instincts and get her out of my life sooner? I thought.'

Lily sighed. 'I'm sure that there are women in the world who are just as devious as men can be when it comes to getting what they want. Maybe she's one of those?'

'I don't doubt you're right. But I still should have been more aware of what she was up to.'

'So you're not having an affair with her, nor rekindling what you had before?' Lily almost held her breath as she waited for his reply.

'You've got to be joking. I've never forgotten the harm she caused me, or the distress. Not to mention her upsetting my father. Is it likely that I'd want her in my life again?'

'No. I don't suppose you would.'

His frown grew a little less anguished. 'Now that I've explained what happened, do you think there's a chance you could learn to trust me again, Lily?'

'I said I didn't trust you in the heat of the moment, when I really believed you were having an affair. But I'm still not happy that you didn't tell me she'd called round and that she tried to kiss you. Is it any wonder that I thought something was going on when you didn't mention her dropping by?'

'I shouldn't have tried to hide the fact. I know that now. I was just trying to save you from being upset and jumping to the wrong conclusion.'

'Which I obviously *did*. Anyway, I'm glad that you've explained. But what hurt me even more, Bastian, was that you thought I'd take the baby away from you. And if that wasn't bad enough, I got the feeling you weren't as worried about losing *me*.'

He was genuinely startled.

Immediately he went to her and drew her up to her feet. 'You've got to be crazy if you believe that for even a second. I *adore* you, Lily—don't you know that by now? I sometimes think I can't breathe without you being near. I don't want anyone else but you. You and our baby are my *life*.'

She was shaking her head and smiling and crying at the same time. 'I can't believe I told you things wouldn't work out between us. I just lost it for a while, I suppose. I can't imagine my life without you, Bastian, and that's the truth.'

'As we're talking about the truth, I don't want you to think I've never made any mistakes in my life, sweetheart. Marissa was a *major* one. I'm no saint.'

'And nor am I. But it's very easy to be fooled by someone—as I know to my cost. You were very young then, Bastian, and no doubt fascinated by a worldly woman like Marissa—and probably flattered, too, that she liked you.'

'Well, now you know I was once capable of being gullible too.' He moved his head disparagingly from side to side. 'And after what that woman did I vowed such a thing would never happen to me again. Thankfully, she taught me a valuable lesson. Anyway, today she exposed her true nature again, when she admitted she's taking her second husband to court for all he's worth and is likely to get it too.' Lowering his voice, he murmured, 'It turns out I had a lucky escape when she cheated on me.'

As his lips twisted wryly the baby in Lily's womb rolled over and, knowing she couldn't have timed it better, she lifted Bastian's hand and placed it on her abdomen.

'*Oddio!*' His dark eyes crinkling delightedly at the corners, he laughed out loud. 'I can feel the baby kicking!'

Smiling, Lily tenderly touched his face. 'It happened for the first time yesterday, when I was loading the washing machine. I jumped into the car and headed straight over to tell you.'

Although he immediately drew her back into his arms, the visible pleasure he'd expressed in feeling the baby move turned into a pained frown. 'And you arrived just in time to see another woman kissing me.'

Releasing a soft breath, she grimaced. 'Let's forget about that now, shall we? I now know that you want us to be together and that's all that matters... You, me and our baby. That's why I married you.'

'If I hadn't already made plans to whisk you off to somewhere especially beautiful for our honeymoon, I would take you into the bedroom and leave you in no doubt that I want you and *only* you, my angel.'

This declaration was followed by several delicious little kisses that inevitably set a flame to Lily's blood and made her want to beg him to do just that. But in the mesmerising haze of his words she found herself returning to what he'd said.

Folding her hands into the front of his shirt, she freed her lips for a moment. 'You said you'd made plans for our honeymoon? Where are we going?'

'I'm taking you to an exquisite hotel on the Adriatic coast, where the guests' privacy is guaranteed to be respected and we won't be troubled by anyone. It's perfect for our honeymoon.'

'It sounds wonderful.'

'I guarantee it will be, *tesoro*.' For a moment his expression was fierce. 'And we won't be in any hurry to get back. Nothing and *no one* will get in the way of our special time together.'

'Oh…'

'Now, do up the top two buttons on your dress, lest it distracts me too much, and go and pack a few clothes.'

In response to the comment Lily widened her green eyes to twin emerald moons. 'What kind of clothes am I going to need?'

His seductive dark gaze sweeping candidly up and down her figure, Bastian replied huskily, 'If I have my way…*not very much…*'

CHAPTER TWELVE

BASTIAN WANTED EVERYTHING to go without a hitch. And as far as their arrival at the hotel and the magnificent suite of rooms they'd been shown into were concerned, everything was flawless—from the wonderful service to the luxurious decor. The attention to detail in every respect was outstanding, and Bastian had stayed in enough such establishments throughout his career to know that this one *more* than lived up to expectations.

However, there was one thing—and without a doubt the most important thing of all—that didn't immediately fall into place. From the moment they arrived he sensed that Lily was uneasy.

Was she still mulling over that unfortunate incident with Marissa?

He hoped not. But she'd suddenly turned quiet, and when he'd asked her a couple of simple questions in Reception she'd flushed even pinker than she usually did, as if drawing any attention to herself was almost painful.

When the immaculate male concierge had finished showing them around their accommodation and wished them a pleasant stay, after generously tipping him Bastian saw him to the door. When he returned it was to find Lily sitting straight-backed in one of the luxurious armchairs.

Lifting her head as if she were in a dream, she remarked woodenly, 'This is really lovely, Bastian.'

'What's wrong?'

'Nothing… Why would you think that?'

'Perhaps because I sense that something is bothering you?'

'I'm fine…'

'Are you? I really want you to enjoy this experience, *amore*. And right now you look as if you'd rather be anywhere else other than here.'

Her pretty face was immediately awash with hectic colour. 'That's not true. It's our honeymoon, remember? Of *course* I want to be here with you, Bastian. It's just…'

'What?'

'Well, it's just that you don't *have* to go out of your way to give me everything you imagine will make me happy. This place is wonderful, but I'd be equally happy *anywhere* if I could just be with you.'

Now it was his turn to colour. It came to him that he was probably trying *too* hard to make everything perfect and not leave anything to chance. And it was having the opposite effect from the one he'd hoped for—which was to let this beautiful woman know that she meant everything to him and he would do anything in his power to have her love and devotion.

The thought of living his life without her was unbearable.

It was then that he realised he echoed her feelings. It wasn't his ability to provide a beautiful place to live nor any of his rich assets that had brought them together. It was a force far greater and more powerful than anything remotely worldly, and Bastian knew unquestionably that they had been destined to find each other...

Going to stand before her, he tenderly helped her up from the chair. His hand cupped the infinitely soft cheek that was already glowing with warmth. 'I have waited for a long time,' he breathed, 'perhaps *too* long to tell you how I feel, *tesoro.* I love you. I love you beyond anything in this world and in the next too. I would lay down my life for you and our children.'

As she let go of her breath, Lily's eyes were moist as her gaze met his. 'I love you too, my darling. I always have and always will. But I was scared to tell you in case it pushed you away from me—in case you thought I was being too possessive.'

'*Never.* My greatest wish has come true in hearing you say that you love me. I swear I will do my utmost for the rest of our lives to make you never doubt that you made the right decision in being with me.'

Their kiss seemed infused with a special kind of magic now. Their breaths became as one as their lips met and drank deeply of each other in a passionate, heartfelt union of body and mind. Finally, his smile rueful, Bastian carefully tipped Lily into his arms and carried her into the sumptuous bedroom.

There was no sense of time passing.

Instead, the seconds, minutes and hours melded into one.

The delicate white voile curtains were moving sinuously in the warm air that drifted in through the open windows and as she lay beneath him on a bed that was covered in voluptuous silks and satins Lily automatically anchored her hands on her lover's shoulders.

They were magnificent—strong and muscular—and they gave her a wonderful sense of being protected, a sense that whatever happened he would be there for her in a heartbeat. They were undeniably sexy too...

Filling her with his hard, scorching heat, Bastian possessed her with dizzying passion. Moving inside her as deeply as he dared, he felt her fingernails bite into his flesh as she began the passionate, irresistible climb to fulfilment. She whimpered her pleasure, moaning low in her throat as she came apart. Bastian followed helplessly.

Breathing hard, they stared at each other in wonder.

Finally, their desire satiated for a while, Lily lay back in his arms and heard his heart beating wildly against her ear. Then she gently pushed aside the recalcitrant lock of hair that brushed his brow and delicately touched her lips to his. But in the next instant his unexpected admission wholly captured her attention.

Winding a strand of her honey-coloured hair round his finger and letting it spring back into a curl, he said, 'You once told me that before you married Marc you'd had no romantic relationships. And that your marriage was never consummated. Is it true, then, Lily, that you must have been a virgin when we first made love? That no man had ever touched you?'

For a second or two all thought was suspended. Then quietly Lily replied, 'It's true. You were my first lover, Bastian.'

With a satisfied sigh she turned and pressed her lips to the masculine chest that was lightly dusted with dark chestnut hair.

Her husband rolled over just then, and carefully took her with him, mindful of the fact that she was carrying their baby in her belly. She helpfully positioned herself more comfortably on top of him and sat astride. The glint in Bastian's eyes instantly revealed his pleasure.

'I'm serious, Lily,' he said. 'Don't you know what a gift that is to give to a man?'

The earnest expression on his handsome

face told her in no uncertain terms just how fervently he meant it.

With a warm glow in her heart, she sighed. 'I'm glad that you feel like that. It makes it even more meaningful that our baby came from our first time together.'

'Yes, it does.'

His sherry-coloured eyes flicked over her, avidly taking in her sexily tousled hair and much fuller pink-tipped breasts.

'Perhaps it's time to drink that toast now? Or before we get round to it my temptation to make love to you again will be impossible to resist.'

She answered the comment with a distinctly cheeky smile. 'Will that be such a hardship, my love?'

She wriggled a little, her satin-textured derriere tauntingly brushing his groin, and he groaned and looked flushed.

'For pity's sake, you know very well it's no hardship, you little witch! But there's a chilled bottle of the finest champagne waiting in the other room. I know you can only have a sip, but I'm a firm believer in celebrating life's important occasions. Trust me—it will be worth it.'

'I'm sure it will, but can't we just enjoy each other for a little bit longer first?'

With a lascivious grin, and pulling her face down to kiss her, Bastian answered, 'You know I can't refuse you anything, my love...'

Standing on their private terrace, gazing out at the crystal blue ocean, Lily couldn't imagine a more breathtaking view. Every arrow of sunlight that pierced the water seemed to leave behind an array of dazzling diamonds. The sight was hypnotising.

Just when she thought it impossible that life could get any better, she sensed the sultry air stir around her and knew that Bastian had joined her.

Approaching her from behind, he lowered his hands to her hips and nuzzled the back of her neck. She was wearing a muslin tunic dress that had a flattering gathered effect around the tummy area, and she was so glad she'd arranged her hair up, on the back of her head, when she'd got dressed.

It gave him much easier access.

'Mmm...' he breathed. 'That's nice...'

Turning round, she kissed him lightly on the mouth. '*You're* nice.'

'I aim to please.'

His smile was both pleased and incorrigible as he fitted her more snugly against him.

'By the way, I'm moving your home office into Buona Stella when we get back. I can't bear for us to be apart for even a moment.'

A series of effervescent tingles—not unlike the sensation she'd felt when she'd had a moderate sip of the champagne—ran up her spine. For the first time the thought of moving into the imposing house with Bastian filled her with genuine excitement.

'Like I told you before, your home is perfect. There's so much space and beauty all around. Our children are going to love living there as they grow up.'

'I trust you will too? I mean, love living there?'

'Do you really need to ask?'

'No, *amore*. You see, I believe we were always meant to be together. Even when I had the house built I prayed someone as good and beautiful as you would come into my life, and the powers that be heard my prayer and generously answered it.'

Lily leant her head back so that she could more easily study him. He wasn't the only one who was blessed. He was a veritable vision of masculine beauty brought to life, she thought, with all the qualities that any woman could want, and she was glad that fate had saved him for *her*.

EPILOGUE

LILY WAS IN the sizeable garden, examining some of the eye-catching blooms, when without warning and out of the blue a sharp pain knifed through her abdomen. It was so painful she abruptly dropped the secateurs she'd been dead-heading the flowers with and clutched at her distended stomach. Another stabbing pain and then another followed, in close succession.

Already three days overdue, Lily knew this must be the start of labour.

Biting her lip and slowly heading back to the house, she was glad that her husband had insisted on working from home these past few weeks—just in case he was needed earlier than they'd anticipated. And being aware that his wife was now overdue had made Bastian even more watchful of her. Knowing that his own mother had died in childbirth, it hadn't been easy for Lily to allay his fears.

Inching her way across the lawn, Lily went inside and reached his study door just as another wave of pain hit. Abruptly coming to a stop, and pushing her long hair behind her ears, she took some deep breaths in and out and schooled herself to try and stay calm.

As if intuiting that she was there, Bastian opened the door, his dark eyes lit with concern. 'What is it? What's wrong?'

Grimacing, she answered, 'I think the baby's coming. My labour pains have started.'

'*Mio Dio!*' His face drained of colour, but he quickly calmed himself and said, 'Then let's make you comfortable while I phone for an ambulance.'

His voice was reassuringly even.

Guiding her to the generous-sized leather couch in his study, he gently lifted her legs up onto the cushions and put the generous-sized pillow he sometimes dozed on when he was working late behind her back.

'Concentrate on your breathing, *tesoro*, and don't worry about anything else,' he advised, smoothing back her hair.

'Easy for you to say!' she quipped, and then

immediately hoped he wouldn't take that the wrong way.

But she didn't even know if he'd heard her. He'd dropped down onto the chair behind his desk, and right then his focus was on ringing for an ambulance.

Minutes later, after relating all the necessary details, he rang off and hurriedly came back to join her. 'The ambulance is on its way. In the meantime, is there anything I can do to help make you more comfortable?'

Swallowing hard, Lily concentrated on her breathing, at the same time anticipating another dizzying wave of pain. But she knew that her love for her husband wouldn't let her forget that he also needed some support during one of the greatest, most life-changing events a couple could have in their lives.

'Yes, my love. You can stay close to me. Then I'll know that everything will be all right.'

'Are you worried that something untoward will happen?'

Bastian couldn't hide the brief flare of fear in his eyes. This was the closest he'd come to confronting one of his darkest terrors. The possibility that Lily—the love of his life—

could die in childbirth, like his mother, tormented him like a cruel enemy he could never vanquish.

Her green eyes glistened. 'Of course not—and nor should *you* be. But that's not to say I won't take some gas and air if the pain gets too—' Her face crumpled and this time it was she who gripped his hand like an iron fist.

He sprang into action, immediately putting his own fears aside and concentrating wholly on helping his wife. 'Breathe deeply, my sweet. That's it. And when the wave comes ride it and all will be well. That's it, my beautiful and strong wife.'

He was mopping her brow with a soft cloth dipped in some cool water when the air was suddenly and abruptly punctuated by the sound of an ambulance siren.

Just a few minutes later they found themselves on their way to the hospital...

Bastian stayed with his wife in the delivery room throughout the birth, feeling his heart pound and his stomach clench at every gutwrenching groan she made, alarmed that she seemed to be suffering so much.

More than once he questioned the obstetrician and the assistant midwife who were in attendance—was the birth progressing normally? But their assurances didn't help as much as he wanted. The spectre of his mother's death in the same situation never left him.

Even Alberto hadn't been able to disguise his concern when Bastian had rung him from the ambulance to tell him that the birth was imminent and that he and Lily were on their way to the hospital.

'How is she, son? She is not in too much distress?' he had asked.

He had glanced down at his wife on the stretcher, where she'd been displaying all the hard-to-bear agony of a woman soon to give birth because her pains had started coming more quickly than she'd thought they would. She'd been gripping his hand hard enough to cut off his circulation.

He'd done his best to stay as calm as he could before answering his father. 'Apart from with the labour pains, you mean? No, Dad. It's just hard to see her suffering so much.'

The line had become tellingly silent for a few moments, and he'd known his father must be reliving what had happened to Bastian's mother after she'd given birth to him. Annalisa had developed a dangerous fever called sepsis and had never recovered.

'Everything is going to be all right, son.'

Coming back to him with renewed resolve in his voice, Alberto had reassured him.

'Lily is a strong woman and she is determined to deliver you a healthy baby. We have talked about it together many times and she has told me how much joy it will bring you both. She loves you so much. History is not going to repeat itself...trust me.'

'Thanks, Dad. I can use all the positive predictions I can get right now.'

'You know I will be there with you in spirit, if not in body, my son, don't you? As soon as we can, after the baby is born, Dolores and I will come to visit. Keep strong, Bastian. You must keep strong for Lily.'

'I will. I don't intend to lose her any time soon. She is *everything* to me.'

There had followed a nail-biting few hours, during which his wife's pain had grown distressing, and her obstetrician had now advised her to take some gas and air.

In between the huge gulps she was taking, Bastian endeavoured to speak calmly to her, keeping his voice low and reassuring, alternately stroking her damp brow and holding her hand. Whatever happened, he vowed to stay with her and watch their baby being born. He was determined that his watchful presence would help Lily and the baby survive, whatever hurdles should face them, no matter how precarious and challenging they might be.

At last the doctor told them that the baby's birth was imminent. Bastian all but held his breath, but he never gave up praying that all would go well. The knowledge that his mother had lost her life in just such a scenario continued to haunt him.

Then, remembering what his father had advised earlier, he knew he had to stay strong. He'd sworn to himself that he wouldn't let Lily down. They were in this together.

'Hold on, my darling,' he told his wife now. 'You're nearly there…the baby is coming.'

He had just seen the baby's head emerging, followed by a sudden rush of arms, torso and legs, and at first sight everything seemed to be in the right place.

When the midwife announced, 'It's a boy, Signora Carrera—you and your husband have a beautiful son!' the infant started to wail loudly and Bastian wanted to laugh and cry at the same time.

Turning to Lily and raining kisses all over her face, he felt beyond elated at the news.

The Carreras had had many discussions around Alberto's kitchen table on naming the new addition to the family, but as yet hadn't decided what that name would be.

Bastian and Lily were the proud and happy parents of a beautiful dark-haired baby boy, and as soon as his wife was up to receiving them there would be a steady line of enthusiastic visitors calling to the house to convey their congratulations. The nursery was all but overflowing with gifts and cards, and Dolores had her work cut out in helping to accommodate them.

One afternoon, after lunch at his dad's place, Bastian stole his wife away from the company for a little while, leaving Alberto and his housekeeper fussing round the infant as he lay in his bassinet. Their son was now three weeks old, and it was seriously bothering him that his first-born was still without a name.

Straight away they went out into the garden, because it seemed a crime to stay inside when it was such a gloriously sunny day. Lily was looking especially beautiful in a pretty blue-and-white dress made from organic cotton. It had a crossover neckline that allowed her to nurse the baby whenever she needed to, and he felt pleased and proud that she wanted to feed the infant herself.

As was often the case, the sight of her immediately drew his thoughts away from everything else and made him focus on *her* instead...

She'd been so brave having the baby. It hadn't been an easy birth, by any means, and at one point the baby had turned over. Bastian was sure he had acquired a few grey hairs before the midwife had turned the infant in the right direction again, but once their son was born Lily had recovered much more quickly than they'd hoped. His beautiful wife was a truly amazing woman, and he didn't care how many times he said so to family, friends and his workers alike.

Catching hold of her slim hands now, he turned up her palms and planted a loving kiss on each one. 'I needed to have you to myself for a while,' he confessed huskily. 'Tomorrow I go back to work, and you will be out of my reach for far too long for my liking.'

'Hmm… Then now is the perfect time to finally decide what our son will be called, don't you think?'

Gazing back into her incandescent green eyes, Bastian knew she had already made up her mind about the name and he braced himself. He hoped that whatever she had chosen wouldn't instigate any disagreement between them. He didn't much care for some of the more quintessentially English names, considering them a bit too 'plummy' for an earthy Italian.

'I can see that you already have a name in mind…am I right?'

'I sometimes think you have a direct line to my thoughts that's almost uncanny…'

'I do—and I'm glad of it. That aside, you'd better tell me what you've chosen.'

'I thought we could name him after one of the Archangels? Raphael is the saint who looks after children and travellers, and it's a beautiful, strong name. What do you think?'

Bastian's lips had already widened into a smile, and this time he kissed Lily full on the mouth to demonstrate his pleasure in her decision. 'It is perfect. I am only annoyed that I didn't think of it myself.'

'But you can live with it? The name, I mean?'

'Raphael Leo Carrera. It is decided. That's our son's name.'

'Where did Leo come from?'

'It came out of the blue just now. Isn't that how we make all our best decisions, *tesoro*? Spontaneously?'

The fair-haired beauty in front of him grinned unashamedly. She knew immediately what he was referring to.

With his arm firmly around her waist, Bastian led his wife back through the open patio doors. 'We shouldn't waste any time before we tell my father and Dolores. Before we know it they'll be organising the baptism.'

'Hold on a minute. Can we just stop for a while?'

'Of course. What is it?'

His wife's lingering gaze all but ate him up.

'I just want to remind you of how much I love you. I don't want you ever to forget that—no matter what challenges we have to face in the future. You and Raphael will be my number one concern—*always*.'

'Along with all the other children we will have?'

'But of course!'

'On that note…'

Instinctively, he moved her against the wall and hungrily closed in on her, feeling her warm breath drift over him, making him ache to get even closer.

'How long before we can…?' Uncharacteristically, he flushed hotly.

'Make love?'

'*Si…*'

'The general advice is to wait until six weeks have passed and the woman has had a chance to heal.'

Bastian huffed out a frustrated breath. 'That means three more weeks, then. I suspect it might be the biggest test of my life!'

'Hmm, but surely it will be worth the wait, my love?'

As she tenderly brushed her lips against his unshaven cheek Lily's smile was unreservedly happy and contented. At last she had found the man she wanted to spend the rest of her life with, and also the place where she wanted to live, with her hopefully growing family, and it was far, *far* better than any idyllic fantasy she could have imagined.

* * * * *

If you enjoyed
CLAIMING HIS PREGNANT INNOCENT
why not explore these other stories
by Maggie Cox?

THE SHEIKH'S SECRET SON
REQUIRED TO WEAR THE
TYCOON'S RING
A TASTE OF SIN
A RULE WORTH BREAKING

Available now!